A scream ripped from her lungs.

"Hang on, Zoe. I'm coming!"

It's not your job. Zoe's voice echoed in his memory. *Your job is to go home safely to your daughters.*

Not till he found her.

Leo bolted up the staircase and found Zoe curled in a ball on the balcony.

"Someone pepper-sprayed me. I can't see." A fit of coughing overtook her.

"It's going to be okay. We'll get you out of here." He looked toward the stairs, but smoke filled the staircase now.

"We have to jump and aim for the lake," Zoe said. "But there's a stone walkway and a wrought iron fence between us and it."

"We have no choice." He swept her up in his arms, stepped onto the railing...and leaped.

It seemed to take forever till she hit water. When she broke through the surface, she saw the castle in flames, but no sign of Leo.

Then she saw the rugged spikes of the fence and his torn uniform hanging from it. And on it was an unmistakable stain. Blood.

Maggie K. Black is an award-winning journalist and romantic suspense author with an insatiable love of traveling the world. She has lived in the American South, Europe and the Middle East. She now makes her home in Canada with her history-teacher husband, their two beautiful girls and a small but mighty dog. Maggie enjoys connecting with her readers at maggiekblack.com.

Books by Maggie K. Black

Love Inspired Suspense

True North Bodyguards

Kidnapped at Christmas
Rescue at Cedar Lake
Protective Measures

Killer Assignment
Deadline
Silent Hunter
Headline: Murder
Christmas Blackout
Tactical Rescue

Visit the Author Profile page at Harlequin.com.

PROTECTIVE MEASURES

MAGGIE K. BLACK

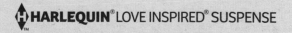

HARLEQUIN® LOVE INSPIRED® SUSPENSE

LOVE INSPIRED BOOKS

Recycling programs
for this product may
not exist in your area.

ISBN-13: 978-0-373-45719-9

Protective Measures

www.Harlequin.com

Printed in U.S.A.

For I am persuaded that neither death nor life, neither angels nor principalities nor powers, neither things present nor things to come...shall be able to separate us from the love of God, which is in Christ Jesus our Lord.
–Romans 8:38-39

Thanks as always to my agent Melissa Jeglinski, my editor Emily Rodmell and the rest of the Love Inspired team for helping me bring these stories to life.

Thank you also to the amazing people at the Harlequin Distribution Center in Depew, NY, who I got the opportunity to visit while writing this book. They ship millions of books a year and are the friendly voices readers hear when they call. For all you do to connect writers to readers, thank you.

ONE

It was a flash of deep red silk that first caught naval commander Leo Darius's attention, followed by a gust of humid air seeping in through one of the balcony doors of the Thousand Islands castle. His steel-gray eyes rose. Their intense gaze cut through the crowded ballroom. But he barely managed to catch a glimpse of the petite, dark-haired woman as she slipped out through the curtains and onto one of the historical building's stone balconies. There'd been no mistaking the outline of a weapons holster strapped to her leg, underneath the folds of her long crimson gown. She was beautiful and dangerous.

But was she carrying the vital military secrets he was there to intercept?

Leo's six-foot frame straightened almost to attention, filling out the crisp lines of his naval dress uniform. He strode across the ballroom, through the flashing cameras, clinking glasses and babble of small talk that filled the room like the thrum of summer bees. A prayer filled his heart. *Please let this hand-off go quickly and smoothly. A whole lot of lives are counting on me.*

It was hard to imagine a mission or battle that was more different to what he was used to. The decorated naval officer had dedicated his life to taking out violent pirates and smugglers on dangerous waters, until the death of his estranged wife, Marisa, had forced him home to raise their two daughters. He'd never expected to be attending events like these, even if it was just as a cover. The weeklong international symposium was supposed to be about celebrating cooperation and hope. Yet, somewhere in all the glitz and glamour was an informant who claimed to be carrying proof that corrupt elements within Canada's own navy had been cooperating with drug smugglers in the North Sea. Leo's mission was simple: find the informant, get the data and analyze whether it was true. He hoped the dazzling stranger was the person he was there to meet. Although he couldn't imagine what kind of woman wore a weapon with evening wear.

"Commander Darius, right?" A male voice with an Irish accent made Leo stop. He turned. Two men stood behind him, both of whom he recognized from the press coverage surrounding the event. The Irishman Killian Lynch was a former wrestling champion turned celebrity journalist. He was in his early thirties, with horn-rimmed glasses perched just above a slight dent on the bridge of an otherwise long and straight nose. The other, Nigel Blackwell, was English, heavier set and an actor who specialized in period dramas. Both men were rising stars and came from countries whose navy patrolled the North Sea.

"It's a pleasure to meet you." Leo shook their hands in turn and exchanged brief introductions. The threat potential of this intel was so high that no one but his own admiral knew of his mission. As far as the gathered guests were concerned Leo was just another delegate. It was a good cover and one that no one would question. Leo was a decorated hero and widower with a picture-perfect family. Not to mention the ability to lock his thoughts and feelings away like a steel trap.

"I've noticed you haven't signed up to take part in the charity auction on Saturday." Nigel's voice boomed with a hint of a chuckle that Leo suspected was practiced. "I will be serving as auctioneer and all the money raised will go to an international charity that builds children's hospitals around the world. I do hope we can count on you."

"Absolutely," Leo said. "Put me down for a meal at one of Ottawa's top restaurants, followed by tickets to the theater." A quick call to the tourism office should sort that quickly enough.

Nigel seemed satisfied with that and wandered off to the dessert table, leaving Leo alone with the Irish journalist.

"I'm surprised you didn't suggest something involving your family," Killian said. "The media are always so eager to get their hands on anything to do with children. Those are your girls, correct?"

Killian gestured to a banner hanging beside the stage. Leo followed his gaze. There alongside banners of the other delegates was a picture of Ivy and Eve, running with him beside the Ottawa River. Blonde and pigtailed, eight-year-old Eve practically bounded off the canvas. But the cautious look in twelve-year-old Ivy's green eyes mirrored the one Leo could feel seeping into his own.

"Yup, they're the genuine article," Leo said. "But

I'm afraid the only event they're taking part in is the parade on Friday." They'd be on a float beside him, visible but protected. Although if all went according to plan the mission would be over by then and he'd be able to skip the rest of the week's events. "Enjoy your evening."

Leo continued across the floor. The curtains billowed slightly. The woman in crimson was still standing on the balcony. She was barely five foot tall, with the lithe build of an athlete and dark, luminous eyes that almost seemed to be looking right at him. Leo felt a hand on his shoulder and realized Killian had followed him.

"Excuse me, Commander," Killian said. "Apologies for being direct, but I don't think you realize the situation you're in."

"And what situation would that be?"

"Clearly you're new to the spotlight." The Irishman's smile was thin. "But there's been a lot of media attention on this conference and the delegates. I put out a call on my website for tips and received several requests for stories about you. Some of them raised the issue of your family situation. I'd be happy to share with you what I've received and even give you an opportunity to review it for your reaction—"

"I don't care about rumors, and I don't read gossip," Leo cut him off. "Marisa was an incredible mother. She passed away unexpectedly last summer from an invasive, malignant cancer. My daughters miss her terribly. Now, if you'll excuse me."

He turned on his heels and strode off. The sooner this mission was over the better. He wasn't cut out for the spotlight. While he didn't know for certain what kind of dirt the man had thought he'd found, he wouldn't have been surprised if someone did the math and realized Ivy had been the result of a teenage pregnancy. Leo had been an emotionally switched off eighteen-year-old, when he'd had a brief relationship with a straight-A student named Marisa, who'd been blinded by a superficial crush on what she imagined might lie beneath his very private shell. The relationship had been a total mistake. Her attraction to him had quickly faded, but not before Ivy was conceived. He'd proposed marriage and joined the navy to support her and the baby. It had been the right decision and one he'd never doubted, even after it had become clear Marisa would never be in love with him. They'd been quietly estranged for years, despite the brief and failed attempt to rekindle a relationship that had resulted in Eve. But the girls had come first. Marisa had been a very protective mother. He wasn't about to let his past become tabloid fodder now.

Meeting his informant and getting the intel safely was all that mattered.

Leo reached the balcony and slid the door open just in time to see the woman in red hop up onto the balcony railing.

"Stop!" He shut the door quickly behind him. "What do you think you're doing?"

She turned and looked at him, her stiletto shoes still a hairbreadth away from the ledge. Wind tossed her black hair around her heart-shaped face. A curious smile turned at the corner of her lips. "Don't worry, Commander. I'm Zoe Dean. It's only about an eight-foot drop and the lawn is pretty soft, especially after the rain. Please, just go back to the party."

Everything about this picture was wrong. She said her name like it should mean something to him, but it didn't, and while he did know someone with the Dean family name, it was the tall, blond linebacker-type who was engaged to Ivy and Eve's therapist, Theresa. Zoe's nose wrinkled, like she was listening to someone talking in a hidden earpiece. She raised her wrist to her mouth and spoke into an intricate bracelet that curled against her skin. "One second, bro. I've got a situation. It's Commander Darius. What do I tell him?"

He glanced over his shoulder. The curtains had closed behind him. Who was this woman? He seriously doubted she was his informant. Yet the idea that she wasn't was even more worrying. If he didn't return to the event, and get back to mingling, he might miss his opportunity to get the drug-smuggling intel. But if the only other option was letting a strange, armed woman skulk around leaping off of balconies, that wasn't any better. *Guide me, Lord.*

"Clearly you know who I am," he said. He stepped toward her. "Which means you know I'm not about to let you hop off over the balcony. So, here's what's going to happen. You're going to get down off that railing and tell me exactly who you are, who you're talking to and what you're doing here."

A gunshot cracked somewhere in the darkness below. Zoe's head spun toward the sound. A cry escaped her lips, as her feet slipped off the crumbling edge of the balcony.

Zoe's hands flailed, grasping at the empty air as she felt her footing give way beneath her. Her body pitched backward. A prayer filled her heart. Then a strong arm slid around her waist, yanking her back onto the balcony. Leo had leaped for her. She clutched at his arm, even as she felt the weight of gravity threatening to pull her from his grasp. A second strong arm went under her knees, as Leo lifted her into his arms and pulled her back against the castle wall, like some kind of knight carrying a damsel to safety. What had just happened? She was a bodyguard, a mixed martial arts specialist and had once been an internationally ranked gymnast. She didn't need some dashing man in uniform to protect her and rescue her from falling. She never had. Yet, here she was in the commander's arms, pressed so tightly against his chest she almost couldn't tell where his heartbeat ended and hers began. "Put me down."

His arms held firm. "Not until you tell me who you are, what you're doing here and why somebody just shot at you."

"I'm pretty sure I wasn't the target," she said. "Sounded like the shot came from somewhere on the grounds below us."

They'd better not have shot at her. Ash Private Security thrived on its secrecy. In the dozens of undercover operations she'd been involved with as a private bodyguard, since helping found the company with her stepbrother, Alex, and their friend Josh, her cover had never once been blown.

"Good news, sis." Alex's voice crackled in her ear. "No imminent danger. No casualties. No reaction from within the party, either. Nothing to worry about. Just looks like the guy we were tracking shot out one of the security cameras in the castle gardens. My best guess is he's heading around the building to one of the side doors, but I can't tell which one. Two security guards are looking for him now, but once he slips inside he could blend in and be anybody. If the commander's still holding you up, I suggest you tell him whatever it takes to get him to let you go."

She looked at Leo. "There's a prowler on the castle grounds, he shot out a surveillance camera in the gardens and security are looking for him now. Check with security and I'm sure they'll say the same."

"That doesn't answer my question," he said.

"I told you, my name is Zoe Dean. My brother, Alex, is engaged to Theresa Vaughan. I spotted a prowler. I can stop him and turn him over to security, but not until you let me go."

Leo brushed her hair away from her face, his finger tracing along the edges of her tiny earpiece. Then his fingers slid over her wrist, holding her hand gently while keeping the microphone in her bracelet away from her lips. His other hand tapped the leg holster strapped to her calf. A shiver ran up the back of her knee. He still hadn't set her down.

"Let me make this very simple," Leo said. "I don't believe you. I've met Alex Dean, and he looks nothing like you. You've got a microphone in your bracelet, you're wearing an earpiece, and unless I'm very much mistaken I can feel a pretty solid leg holster on your calf. Knife, though, not gun, so at least that's one law you're not breaking. So either you come up with a much more convincing story than that or I'll have you arrested."

"Is that a challenge?" she asked.

He grinned, but only slightly like he couldn't help himself.

"Then let me make one thing clear," she said. "The only reason I didn't go for a quick, sharp jab to your windpipe and leave you here gasping for breath, is because you're very respected by a couple of people who I'd give my life for and I promised them I wouldn't cause a disturbance."

"Really?" His dark eyebrows rose.

"Yes, really," she said. It seemed like he was determined to doubt her. "Do you want me to prove it to you? When you were serving in the Middle East, you transported a soldier on one of your missions called Joshua Rhodes. Josh tipped you off about a drug smuggler in your crew and you had the smuggler dishonorably discharged." Leo's face paled. The skeptical grin faded. Yeah, she imagined he could count on one hand the number of people who knew that story. But she wasn't done. "When you returned to Canada, a year ago, Josh gave you a call and told you that his good friend Alex had gotten engaged to an amazing psychotherapist named Theresa, who specialized in child trauma. He said that she lived near Toronto but was willing to drive out to Ottawa to see your daughters, if you thought it would help them. Josh is my colleague. Alex is my colleague and my stepbrother—we both lost a parent when we were young. Josh, Alex and I are bodyguards for a very private and elite firm called Ash Private Security."

Leo's grip loosened. She slipped from his arms and landed on her feet on the balcony.

"Talk about pulling out the big guns," Leo said. "You could've just told me you worked with Josh."

He was rattled. She couldn't blame him. She'd been warned that Leo was a very private man, and here she'd just rattled off two rather personal things about him that she guessed not many people knew.

"I honestly didn't think you'd believe me, and I didn't want to hang around here trying to convince you." An unexpected flush rose to her cheeks. He would hardly be the first person to underestimate her or presume someone her size couldn't protect lives. But was he always this suspicious? He was easily one of the most skeptical people she'd ever met. "When you're my size you learn to make your first shot a big one, as it might be the only one you get."

His eyebrow rose. "Like taking on a prowler and leaping off a balcony."

"I was a nationally ranked gymnast growing up and I competed internationally in mixed martial arts until I was fifteen," she said. "And yes, I work with Josh and Alex—as a bodyguard. Theresa consults for Ash, too, on occasion, and Josh's wife, Samantha, sometimes helps with online research. In fact, I'm the only member of the team who didn't get an invite to this shindig. But since Josh and Samantha are on their honeymoon, Theresa's back home in Toronto seeing clients and Alex is outside manning the surveillance van, I got to be the person on the inside. I trust you won't blow my cover."

She might no longer be in his arms, but she was still standing so close to him she could almost feel him against her chest. She held her breath still half expecting him to tell her that she didn't look like a bodyguard.

Instead Leo asked, "Who's your client?"

"I'm here on surveillance only." She took a step back. "A couple of our clients have been targeted by a particularly nasty gang of thieves. Samantha picked up some online chatter that three of them would be here tonight scoping out a new target. So, I'm here to hunt the potential thieves while they stalk their next target." She took another step backward.

Leo's arms crossed in front of his chest. "You knew thieves were targeting an international gala and you didn't alert the police or security?"

"Of course we did," she said. "But this particular group of thieves don't pick pockets and grab handbags. They think of themselves as vigilantes, who in their own twisted logic are righting wrongs and meting out justice. They steal big things, like companies and identities. They plan stings that take months, to break into vaults or invent media scandals. Are you familiar with Greek mythology?"

He shook his head. "Let's say I'm not."

"They call themselves The Anemoi." She pronounced it like "the enemy." "Which roughly means a group of deadly storms. That's what these thieves do. They destroy lives and leave them in ruins. They've targeted three of our clients so far, nobody has ever successfully identified a single member of their gang and the police seemed convinced they're a myth. Internet chatter that three of them were here tonight, scoping out their next target, was too good an opportunity to pass up, and I'm not about to stand around and try to convince you they're real when one is sneaking around the gardens as we speak." She took another step back, sweeping her long skirt into her hand. "It really was a pleasure to meet you, Commander. I hope you enjoy your evening."

"Wait!" Leo said. He was too late. She'd already vaulted backward, over the balcony.

She landed on the grass and rolled, feeling the soft damp earth absorb the blow. Then she sprang back up into a crouching position. She raised her bracelet microphone to her lips. "Okay, Alex, I'm down in the garden. Tell me you've still got eyes on our guy."

"No, I don't and security doesn't have him, either." Alex's voice was in her ear. "Please tell me you didn't just leap off the balcony."

"He was frowning at me, and I didn't want to waste time arguing with him."

"Or climbing down safely. Or taking the stairs."

She slipped into the shadows against the stone wall as her eyes scanned the night around her. Heavy iron fence lay to her right. Beyond it swirled the dark waters of the Saint Lawrence River. She headed left, toward the front of the building, following the path as it curved around flowers and fountains. "Just tell me what he looks like."

"Samantha's intel said there are three Anemoi thieves on-site tonight," Alex said. "They go by the handles Prometheus, Pandora and Jason. Prometheus stole fire from Mount Olympus. Pandora opened a box that shouldn't be opened. But Jason is a weird code name for a criminal."

"Jason of the Argonauts stole a golden fleece," Zoe said.

"Got it. Based on my intel, the guy skulking around the gardens is Prometheus. He's really big with broad shoulders. Imagine a bull in a jumpsuit."

"You hate being stuck in the van, don't you?" she asked.

"At least Theresa's happy I'm keeping out of danger." He laughed. "Just wait until I tell her she missed hearing you flirt with the great Commander Darius."

"We weren't flirting." She felt herself blush. Maybe the good-looking commander had taken her breath away, just a little. But Leo was a valiant and decorated national hero. She was just a bodyguard. Not to mention, he was also a devoted father. And she'd always suspected she wasn't cut out for motherhood, even before a doctor had confirmed she'd never be able to have children of her own.

A man like him wouldn't be drawn to a woman like her.

"Next time we have a mission like this, you can wear the fancy clothes and I'll stick to blue jeans," she added. She took one last glance back at the balcony. It was empty. Leo hadn't come after her. But at least he hadn't blown her cover. A long, thin braided belt skimmed the waist of her gown. She looped her fingers through it and with a quick tug, her long skirt pleated neatly into a knee-length tunic. She had matching athletic shorts on underneath. Ta-da. Bit of Samantha's creative tailoring and she'd just gone from gown to something she could actually move around in.

"Is he as handsome in person as the media makes him out to be?" Alex asked.

She rolled her eyes and ignored his teasing.

A life in competitive sports, not to mention a string of unrequited teenage crushes, had taught her pretty quickly that there were two kinds of guys in the world. Those who viewed her as equal and were happy to fight alongside her, but saw her as nothing more than one of the guys. And those who saw her as a "girl."

They were an even bigger problem. Something about her threatened them, she supposed. All she knew was that too many of them had the urge to cut her down to size. A sly word here, a crude gesture there, the occasional demeaning comment when nobody was looking, day after day, from creep after creep, until she'd eventually snapped when she was fifteen, spun around and elbowed the offending guy in the face, not even registering that the camera was rolling. That had been the end of her competing internationally. Now that creep, Killian Lynch, was a famous face in the spotlight and she slunk in the shadows.

"You okay?" Alex asked. It was impossible to hide anything from him.

"Yeah, I'm fine." She paused. The path ahead curved into a bridge over an ornamental pond. She started toward it. "But I saw Killian Lynch."

The fist seemed to shoot out of nowhere as a black-clad figure leaped from the darkness. His arm swung toward Zoe's face, giving her just seconds to dodge the blow as it flew inches from her jaw. She spun toward her attacker. Alex hadn't been exaggerating— the man was huge, with a flat face that looked like it had been in too many fights. Her hands rose as years of competitive training coursed like adrenaline in her veins. But she barely had a second to catch her breath before a knife flashed in the moonlight.

"Found Prometheus!" She leaped back again as the blade swung inches away from her stomach. "He's got a knife."

"Do you need backup?"

"I might." Her attacker slashed again. This time she ducked under the blade, then with a quick flick of her wrists snapped the knife from his fingers. She heard it clatter in the darkness. Prometheus kicked the legs out from under her. She stumbled. Her stiletto heel snagged on the cobblestone. She pitched into a protective front roll, a sinking sensation filling her stomach as she felt the path disappear beneath her. She tumbled into the flower pond. Muddy water engulfed her body. She scrambled out again. Prometheus was gone.

"I lost him." She yanked off her stilettos. Nonsense like this was why she hated working in fancy clothes. Her bare feet ran quickly and silently down the path. A utility door was open on her right. "Found an open door. He must be inside. He won't get far."

She slipped through the door. Air-conditioning raised goose bumps on her skin. She was in a historical gallery of some sort with flat glass cases and the eerie blue glow of dim emergency lights. "I'm going to keep trailing him. Okay, Alex… Alex?"

Silence from her earpiece. No typing. No static. No buzz.

No Alex.

Her earpiece must've shorted out when she hit the water. *Help me, Lord. I'm on my own.* Footsteps echoed in the distance. She sprinted through the hall and into another almost identical one, just in time to see the black-clad figure dart into a side door. The door slammed behind him. She yanked the knob. It was locked.

Nah, he wasn't getting away that easily. She pulled a bobby pin from her hair, snapped it in half and went to work picking the lock. Beyond the door she could hear the clatter of things falling over and furniture being moved. Sounded like he was tossing the place. She whispered a prayer and focused on the lock. Then the floorboards creaked behind her. She spun. Her hands rose to strike. But a strong hand intercepted her blow, catching her small hand in his, and holding it firmly before she could pull it back.

"Nice punch." It was Leo.

"Nice block." She blinked and looked up at the tall, handsome uniformed officer. "What are you doing here?"

"I ran down the back stairs."

"Now where's the fun in that?" The words slipped out of her lips before she'd stopped to think.

He chuckled. It was a deep, warm laugh that seemed to rumble from somewhere inside his chest. Heat was rising to her face again, and it didn't help that he still hadn't let go of her hand. "Well, after your rather dramatic exit, I went straight to the head of security and told him I thought I'd heard a bullet fired in the castle gardens. I then asked him point-blank if there was an intruder on the grounds. Do you know what he told me? He said all I'd heard was a car backfiring, not to worry and I should get back to the party." Leo took a step back and pulled his hand from hers. "Then I spoke to a high-ranking police officer, who I casually know, and asked if he'd ever heard of The Anemoi. He laughed very loudly and told me The Anemoi was a myth."

Zoe's heart sank.

His hand slid into his jacket pocket and pulled out a cell phone. "Then, I sent a quick text to my old friend Josh Rhodes, even though I knew full well that he's on his honeymoon, and asked him if he'd ever even heard of you. You can imagine how I felt when he texted back immediately, 'She's one of ours. Believe whatever she tells you. Do whatever she says.'"

A smile of relief brushed Zoe's lips. Was it her imagination or was the air between them growing warmer? Leo took another step back. Then, for the first time, his gaze seemed to take her all in. His eyebrows rose. "What happened to you?"

"I found the intruder that security told you doesn't exist," she said. "He had a knife. We fought. I disarmed him. But he knocked me into a pond. Then he ran through that door."

He reached past her for the door handle. Then winced. "It's hot. Stand back."

She stood back. He leveled one strong kick at the door that sent it flying back off its hinges.

She turned. Sudden white-hot fear shot up her spine. The room was on fire.

TWO

Heat hit Leo's body like a wave. Flames climbed the curtains of the coat-check room and spread out across the ceiling. Coats burned. Briefcases and laptop bags buckled in the heat. Dark smoke billowed toward them. His heart stopped. Every single piece of paper or electronic data that had been left in that room was being reduced to ashes. If the thief had stolen something, the fire would probably destroy any possibility of figuring out what it was. Had the thieves Zoe had been tracking either stolen or destroyed the intel he was after?

If so, the implications of what that could mean were positively terrifying. Leo had made one other phone call on his rapid descent down the stairs to the one person inside the navy he trusted, his superior, Admiral Jacobs. Jacobs hadn't answered, and the last voice mail message he'd left for Leo hadn't changed. The informant said they would be at the party. Their identity was still unknown, but Leo was authorized to wire them up to a quarter of a million dollars if the intel proved true. He glanced at the ceiling. "No sprinklers and no fire alarm."

"There's a fire extinguisher on the other side of the cloakroom." Zoe's voice came from behind him.

"It's too late for that. We have to evacuate the building." Wrapping his jacket around his hand, Leo grabbed the handle and yanked the door closed. "This fire door should help contain it long enough to evacuate. But we won't have long. Get out of the building. Get a safe distance away, then call 9-1-1."

Leo pressed his cell phone into her hand. She took it. Then her eyes closed for a fraction of a second and he watched as a prayer moved on her lips. Then she looked up at him. Fear was creeping in the edges of her eyes, but it did nothing to dim the determination burning within them. She gave him a push. "I'm on it. Just go. I'm right behind you!"

He ran through the hall, into a second almost identical one, and then burst through another door into the lobby. The English actor Nigel was standing by the front desk talking to an elderly security guard. They both looked up.

"The coat-check room is on fire," Leo said. "Sprinklers aren't working. We need to evacuate the building. I'll get the ballroom. You clear the staff and the main floor. Now!"

He pelted up the winding staircase to the second-floor ballroom without waiting for a response. He hit the second-floor ballroom. Well-dressed people packed the room. Waitstaff weaved between them. His eyes scanned the room in an instant, trying to access the best way to evacuate without causing a panic. The last thing he wanted was to cause a stampede.

"Emergency services are on their way!" Zoe ran past him barefoot, like a tiny bolt of lightning. "Alex is trying to get the sprinklers back online. There's a small lounge and balcony upstairs. I'll go evacuate them while you sort out down here."

She disappeared up a second smaller set of stairs. His head shook. That woman was unbelievable. He'd told her to escape the building and instead she was running right into danger. He strode across the floor to the stage and up to the podium, feeling the old, familiar authority with which he'd commanded battleships slipping around him like a mantle. He reached the microphone and tapped it twice. No sound. But, one glance at the man behind the sound board and it sprang to life.

"Ladies and gentlemen, your attention, please." His voice filled the room. "Sorry to interrupt the party, but there is a small contained fire in a separate section of the building downstairs. Emergency services are on their way. What I need you to do is to just calmly walk downstairs and wait outside on the grass, so they can come in here and do their jobs." Voices began to babble. Questions rose around him. He raised his hand. "We can all talk outside. But right now, I need you to exit the building. Quickly and quietly. Go."

The babbling grew louder. But he also caught the eyes of a handful of men and women, who he could tell at a glance had also served their country and community in one way or another and knew how to handle a crisis. They started ushering those around them toward the staircase. Guests started filing down the stairs. People in kitchen uniforms and waitstaff poured out side doors. Still others streamed down from the floor above. The hall began to clear. He breathed a sigh of relief and a prayer of thanksgiving. The fire door wouldn't hold forever. But he had hope the building would clear before the fire spread. He walked back to the stairs and positioned himself on the landing to direct traffic, until finally the trickle of people heading out the doors stopped.

But where was Zoe?

He started back across the now empty ballroom to the stairs he'd seen her run up. The smell of smoke grew heavier in the air. Then he saw a waiter—tall and thin with long blond hair and goatee—kneeling on something behind the stage.

"Hey!" Leo ran toward him. "You need to get out of here!"

The waiter didn't move. Instead he grabbed a phone from his pocket and took a picture of whatever was on the floor.

"This isn't a drill." Leo grabbed the man's shoulder. "The building's on fire!"

The waiter leaped up and wrenched his shoulder away from Leo's grasp. Then he spun toward Leo and through the smoky air Leo could barely make out the shape of something long and black in his hand. The waiter lunged toward him. A knife? A gun? A Taser? Leo had only seconds to react as he knocked it free from the man's hand. It was a thick black marker. And for the first time Leo saw what he had been kneeling on. It was the banner of him and his girls. Ugly black marker lines crossed the canvas, slashing the picture in between Leo and his daughters, and severing the connection between his hand and Eve's.

"What do you want?" Leo demanded. "Who started the fire? What's the meaning of this?"

A scream split the smoke-filled air. It was Zoe.

The sound of fear and pain that ripped from her lungs seemed to tear his own chest in two. The waiter slithered away and pelted for the stairs.

"Zoe! Hang on, I'm coming!" Leo ran across the ballroom and up the narrow flight of stairs that led up to the third floor. A woman was tearing down the stairs toward him. It was a waitress in black pants and a crisp black shirt. Long, unnaturally bright red hair fell over her shoulders. He barely managed to stop as she nearly collided with him. "What happened? Why is my friend screaming?"

The waitress's violet eyes widened. But she shoved past him and ran down the stairs without answering.

"Leo! Help!" Zoe was calling his name. His heart wrenched toward the sound.

"Hold on, I'm coming!" Leo bolted up the narrow staircase to the top floor. It was small, with slanted ceilings and doors in all directions. He followed the sound of her voice, burst through another door and ended up outside on a patio. Humid air surrounded him. But it was the faint cloud of pepper still hanging in the air that made his eyes sting and his heart ache. "Zoe? Where are you?"

"I'm here!" A sob choked in her voice. He glanced around. A coffee cart had been knocked over. Broken dishes littered the ground. Then he saw her. Zoe was curled in a ball against the low wall. He dropped to his knees beside her.

"A waitress pepper-sprayed me." Thick tears streamed down Zoe's face. "I can't see a thing."

Leo's blurred shape floated before her stinging eyes. Zoe blinked rapidly, trying to wash away the pain. "I cleared the place out, but this one waitress just wouldn't leave."

"Did she have red hair?" he asked. "Purple eyes?"

"Wig and colored contacts, yeah," she said. A fit of coughing overtook her lungs. The burn of the pepper spray seared in her throat. Fresh tears blurred her vision.

"Hey," Leo said softly. "It's going to be okay. We're going to sort your eyes and get you out of here safely. I promise."

She felt his hands brush the sides of her face. He tucked her hair behind her ears.

"Wow, you really did take the blast full on, didn't you?" He whistled softly under his breath. "I've seen men four times your size fall apart from way lighter blasts than that."

She could tell he was trying to make her feel better. Somehow it helped.

"I shouldn't have tried to force her to leave," she said. "It was clear she was up to something. Alex told me The Anemoi crew had a woman on it. Her handle is Pandora. It was probably her. I don't know why I didn't just leave her and then run."

"Because that's not who you are. Even I know that." He pulled a white handkerchief from his breast pocket and drenched it in milk from the coffee tray. Gently, he placed the handkerchief against her stinging skin. She almost gasped in relief. "Hold this to your face. It'll help until we can flush your eyes out with water. Now, I'm going to pick you up and carry you out of here."

Her chin raised. "I can walk."

"You'll bump into things."

"Not if you guide me."

He took her other hand and helped her to her feet. She followed him back into the building. Heavy smoke filled her senses. Then she felt him stop. She dropped the handkerchief from her eyes but saw nothing but a wall of gray.

"Can't take the stairs, the fire's spread to the second floor," Leo said. Then she heard him pray for guidance.

"We'll have to jump and aim for the river," Zoe said. "It's pretty deep. But there's a stone walkway and a wrought iron fence between us and it."

"How far out is it?" he asked.

"Six feet maybe," she said. "I can jump it."

"Not without your eyes," he said. "Sorry, but I think we're going to have to make this jump together."

He swept her up into his arms. Then she felt him run, pelting out across the patio. The sizzle of the fire echoed behind them. The wail of distant sirens filled the air.

Help us, Lord. Please, help us.

She felt him take a step up onto the balcony railing. He leaped and they were airborne. They fell through the air. Her head pressed against his chest. His strong arms locked around her. She took a breath and prepared to hit the water. But then suddenly something jerked them backward. Then she felt him throw her forward, launching her out of his arms. Her body smacked the water. She went under and opened her eyes but saw nothing but the green-gray wall of murky water. She kicked hard and swam for the surface, blinking rapidly as she felt the sting of the pepper spray flush from her eyes. Chaos reigned around her. The castle was a wall of flame casting the scene in an eerie red glow. Sirens wailed closer. People crowded around the fence, yelling, pointing, and it took her a breath to realize she was what they were looking at.

"Leo? Where are you?" Desperately her blurry gaze scanned the surface of the water. Where was he? Why had he thrown her like that? Then she saw the segment of fence had caved in and broken off. Jagged spikes of what remained jutted out over the water. His torn jacket hung like a rag from one of the barbed points. She swam toward it. Ash and debris rained down around her. Panic filled her core.

Lord, where was he? Please, may he be okay.

Then she saw the air bubbles streaming up from beneath her. She gasped a deep breath and dove under again, feeling for him through the darkness. Thick seaweed grabbed at her body. Her lungs ached for breath. Then she felt him, thrashing in the water beneath her, caught on a portion of fallen fence. She reached for him but was almost flung back by the force of his arm. She gritted her teeth and swam forward again.

It's okay. I've got your back, Commander. Let me help you. Her fingers felt for his arm. Then she felt his hand grab hers and squeeze. She yanked the knife from her leg holster and pressed it into his palm. He took it. She swam upward, praying with each stroke to feel him following her. She broke through the water and gasped for air. Leo surfaced beside her.

"Thank you!" He gulped a deep breath. Water streamed down the strong lines of his jaw. "You saved my life."

"You saved mine." Then she heard the rumble of

debris rushing down toward them. He yanked her into his arms and sheltered her body with his as the flaming balcony caved in toward them.

THREE

It was like swimming through a minefield in a hurricane. Thick smoke filled the air. The heat was like a shimmering wave in the darkness. Falling bricks and rock crashed down around them, churning the water and threatening to crush them alive. But in the midst of it all she felt Leo's strong arm around her, sheltering her from the crumbling building as it collapsed in flames and rubble around them. Zoe swam upstream, her strong legs kicking for her life against the current, only vaguely aware of the voices yelling somewhere beyond her in the chaos. They cleared the debris, but kept swimming, upstream, letting the crowd and fire fade behind them.

The air cleared. Then Leo stopped swimming, took her hand and pulled her into a bay. Rock rose sheer and high beside them. She tried to stand, but the tips of her toes barely brushed the bottom.

"Are you okay?" he asked.

She nodded, treading water. "Yeah, I'm okay. You?"

"Yep." He slid her utility knife back into her hand. "Thank you for coming after me. I was good and stuck there for a moment."

She took the knife and traded him for his cell phone, hoping for his sake it was waterproof. Behind them the fire raged, lights from what looked like an endless stream of emergency vehicles flashed and spun, and silhouettes of people crowded the shoreline.

"We should go," she said. Her eyes searched the rock for handholds. "I have to find Alex and I imagine a lot of people will be looking for you."

"Hang on." He reached for her hand. "Just one second. We need to talk."

Here and now? In a river?

"Okay," she said. "But let's get out of the water first and talk on the dry land. It's so deep, I can't even stand here."

But instead, he pulled her closer until she was standing on her tiptoes on top of his boots.

"You're right, people will be looking for us," Leo said. His hand slid around her back, holding her firm, even as she could feel the current beating against their bodies. "But we need to talk alone, without an audience, and the moment I get to shore I'll be swamped by people again. So please, quickly, tell me everything you know about The Anemoi."

The intensity in his voice rattled something inside her. There was an urgency there that she hadn't heard before. Had he been The Anemoi's target? Did he know something about The Anemoi or the fire that he wasn't telling her? She could feel his hand on the small of her back and the strength of his arms under her fingers. This man had saved her life. She had saved his. Yet, he was still virtually a stranger and she was still on a mission.

"Okay," she said. "I'll give you five minutes, but

then I'm climbing out of this river. Also, I'm talking to you off the record. None of this goes to the press. None of this gets repeated as gossip. Okay? I'm trusting you here."

"Yeah, I got it," he said. "I'm good at keeping secrets and I can't abide gossip. You can trust me."

She took a deep breath and hoped that was true.

"Two months ago, a client contacted us saying his identity had been stolen and his bank accounts emptied," Zoe said. "Police had no leads. We said we'd look into it, but honestly didn't expect to find much. We're a private security firm, not detectives. Then, three weeks later someone else called us claiming to be the victim of a grand conspiracy to ruin his reputation."

"And you saw a connection?" Leo asked.

"Samantha did," Zoe said. "She's brilliant when it comes to online research and making connections. She started digging into something called the Dark Web and building these info charts, before finally hitting on The Anemoi. Basically, they're a bunch of loosely connected crooks that steal very important things for people, for a very high price. They tend to go by handles from Greek mythology. Like, the guy who attacked me with the knife calls himself Prometheus after the Titan who stole fire from Olympus. In their twisted minds they're convinced they're the good guys, righting wrongs and wrecking lives they think deserve to be destroyed."

Leo blew out a long breath. She waited. When he didn't say anything more, she kept going.

"I get how ridiculous it probably sounds," she said, "that there are these people, who are fooling themselves into thinking they're some kind of heroes when they're really just criminals being paid a whole lot of money to utterly ruin people's lives."

"In my experience most criminals tend to be pretty delusional and think that they're justified," Leo said. "Nobody wants to believe they're the bad guy."

She smiled. Okay, maybe he was the kind of person she could talk to. At least it seemed like he was taking her seriously.

"There were three of them at the gala tonight," she said. "Their code names were Prometheus, Pandora and Jason. I guess Pandora pepper-sprayed me. I never saw Jason, but apparently he's young, tall and thin. Like I told you, Samantha saw some online chatter about them scoping out a potential target at this gala and I went in undercover to see if I spotted anything fishy or could identify any members of the team. Something we could pass to police to help our current clients or even help us be on the lookout for the future. I have no idea why they'd set the coatroom on fire, unless it's to keep someone from discovering what they've stolen or rifled through. We have no idea who their target is or what they're attempting to steal. It could be something professional or intensely personal."

There was another long pause. Again, she couldn't shake the idea that he knew something he wasn't telling her. This time she waited Leo out. Finally he said, "How do they usually warn their targets?"

"What?" She nearly slipped off his toes and into the water. "They don't warn them. At least, I've never heard of anyone from The Anemoi warning anyone. Why?"

She waited again. But this time Leo didn't answer.

"Leo?" Her tone grew sharper. "What do you know that I don't?"

"Don't worry about it. I saw a thin man—could be Jason—defacing a poster in the ballroom. But it might not mean anything."

He was talking like it was no big deal, but that didn't explain why his voice sounded both angry and strangled.

"Do you think you know who the target was?" she asked. No answer. A chill ran down her spine. "Could it be you? Do you have something worth stealing?"

"No, I don't," he said.

Why didn't she believe him? Voices were clamoring above them now. People were running toward them.

"We've got some survivors over here!" a male voice bellowed above her. "Can someone grab us a rope?"

She looked up and was blinded by the glare of flashlights. Leo pulled her against the rock.

"I'm going to hoist you up," he said. "You should be able to climb up from there. It's not that far."

Light fell from above, highlighting the lines of his chiseled jaw and the strength that lay beneath his wet dress shirt. But it was the depth of the worry pooling in his eyes that made her heart stop beating.

"What's wrong?" Her hand brushed his jaw. "Tell me. Do you have any reason to believe you're The Anemoi's target? Is there anything you have that someone would think shouldn't belong to you?"

To her surprise, he hugged her quickly with the shared relief of two people who'd been through trauma together. She hugged him back.

"Don't worry about me." Leo's voice was a deep, gruff whisper in her ear. "I don't have anything worth stealing, and definitely nothing that a vigilante would argue doesn't belong to me. Thank you for everything."

He hoisted her up. Other hands were reaching down for her. She stepped up onto Leo's shoulder and grabbed onto one of the outstretched hands. A police officer pulled her up onto the ledge.

"Are you alright, miss?" a paramedic asked. There was a light in her still sensitive eyes. He took her arm and started leading her toward a bank of ambulances.

"I'm fine, thank you." She pulled away.

The paramedic let her go without an argument. She wasn't surprised considering the scene. Firefighters and emergency service personnel were trying to corral people, put out the fire and check for injuries. Party guests rambled around the gardens, ignoring orders and trying to take pictures on their phones.

She'd learned as a teenager that whenever there was a spectacle there'd be two different types of people running around. There were those who watched the show and those who kept people safe. Back then she'd been the spectacle, the fire, the flashy and fierce marital arts and gymnastics competitor who people cheered for loudly when she won and booed at when it all came to an end. But she'd known, even then, what kind of person she wanted to be. She wanted to be the one who protected people and rescued them from the metaphorical flames.

The crowd parted and she saw Leo hauling himself over the ledge. He stood on the edge of the rocks, with the fire to his right, the darkness to his left and the river swirling behind him. Her breath caught in her throat. He was rugged, strong and dashing in a way she'd thought only movie stars could be. Yet as his eyes scanned the crowd, something deep inside his gaze almost looked wounded, too.

Lord, protect him and help him. I don't know what he wasn't telling me or why he brushed off my questions. Or why my gut's telling me that he was The Anemoi's intended target.

The Anemoi had gotten its name from a group of deadly winds, and somehow the castle fire felt like the first rumble of thunder that warned of an approaching storm. Something big was coming. Something devastating and dangerous. And she just couldn't shake the feeling that Leo Darius was going to be right in the center of that storm.

People pushed past her. Voices babbled around her, fading into white noise. Still her eyes were locked on Leo's form. He'd come for her. He'd carried her in his arms. He'd leaped through the air to save them both. She'd trusted him with the truth about her job at Ash Private Security and about The Anemoi. But he hadn't trusted her in return.

"Excuse me! Ma'am." The Irish voice was smooth behind her and his hand touched her shoulder so suddenly she nearly jumped out of her skin. She flinched, her whole body pulling away as she turned. It was him, Killian, the same creep who used to skulk around the edges of martial arts competitions hitting on the female competitors, until one day, when he'd snuck up behind her, she'd wielded around and elbowed him in the face on live television, ending her competitive career. "Are you the woman who Commander Darius rescued from the fire?"

She nearly choked. He didn't recognize her. She didn't know if it was just because of the odd way the combination of the night, the flames and emergency beams played tricks with light and shadows. Or if it was because of how disheveled she was from the fire and the lake.

But she couldn't shake the thought that maybe he'd actually forgotten her. That despite everything she'd lost by elbowing him in the face, she'd been nothing but an insignificant and forgettable blip in his life.

Even though she'd never forgotten his face.

"No comment." Zoe didn't meet his eye and turned away, hoping not to jog his memory.

"No comment?" he pressed. "How can you have no comment? Either you're the woman he rescued or you're not."

"Sorry, I've got to go." She persisted through the crowd, searching the sea of emergency vehicles for the plain black Ash Security van.

Killian kept following her. She could hear his voice as sharp and direct as arrows shooting after her. "At least, tell me your name. Who are you?"

"I'm nobody." She disappeared into the crowd. She was nobody now. She liked it that way. One brief intense encounter in a moment of danger with the daring Commander Leo Darius wasn't about to change that.

The Ottawa River raged and surged as it flowed through Canada's capital city, past beautiful historical buildings and stately monuments. Leo walked with his daughters down a path that ran alongside one of the river's branches as it flowed into a canal. His mind swirled like the water. It was Tuesday, the morning after the fire. Thankfully no one had been hurt, the symposium was continuing as usual and the informant had left another untraceable robotic message on Leo's phone line saying the intel was still up for sale but the price had just gone up. But an early morning phone call from Admiral Jacobs's secretary had sent everything into chaos. The admiral had been in a terrible car accident on the way to work and was now in the hospital. Leo had no way to get the admiral's advice on whether he should continue with the mission, no idea who could've tipped The Anemoi off to the informant's existence and no one else inside naval intelligence he knew he could trust. He was on his own. His eyes rose to the sky in prayer. *I just don't know what to think. I don't know what to do. Guide me. I need backup and I don't know how to get it.*

"Can I get ice cream?" Eve's voice broke into his thoughts. Bright blue eyes looked up hopefully into his. Her tiny hand slipped into his large one and squeezed it, very hard, like she was double-checking he was really there. "Or can I climb a tree?"

There was something so real and genuine about his littlest girl's smile.

Thank You, God, for my daughters. Help me be the father they need me to be. Help me raise them and protect them.

"You can't climb a tree in flip-flops," he said. "But we can see about ice cream later."

Eve squeezed his hand hard one more time. Then she scampered off to join her sister, Ivy, who was now walking alone up the path ahead of them. Ivy had been a little girl on his last visit home. Now, at twelve, she was almost a teenager, with long hair as dark as his and eyes that tended to glance sideways at the world. He watched as Eve nudged her big sister in the side. Ivy threw her arm protectively around Eve's shoulders.

It was hard to know how much the strained mess that was his marriage to their mother had impacted them, but he knew they missed her. He missed Marisa, too, in a much more complicated way. Late at night, her painful words to him still echoed in the empty recesses of his chest: "I tried to love you, Leo. I really did. You're just not the kind of man who's easy to love." But she'd stayed married to him, accepted politeness instead of romance, made a bed for him on the couch whenever he was home on leave and given him two beautiful daughters. He'd always be thankful for that.

"This isn't really a normal walk, Eve," Ivy said, in a conspiratorial tone that was so loud she had to know that he would be able to hear it. "Daddy is meeting someone. But it's a secret meeting."

Eve gasped, a sound that was thankfully all excitement and intrigue, not worry. Leo almost stopped short. How could she possibly know that? Josh had phoned his cell before the sun had risen this morning to suggest they meet up. Josh's tone had been friendly, but there'd been a current cutting through it that had let him know it was important. Leo kept his voice level. "Why do you say that, honey?"

"I'm right, aren't I?" Ivy tossed a glance back over her shoulder. A slight smile turned at her lips, her keen eyes flashed and he realized that she'd been guessing. She was a smart kid and perceptive, too. Neither of which helped the gnawing feeling he got in his gut sometimes that Ivy was bothered about something she still didn't trust him enough to open up about.

His cell phone buzzed. He reached for it hoping it was the admiral. Instead it was a text from a number with an Irish area code.

Hey Commander, it's Killian Lynch. Any news on the identity of your mystery woman? My message board's been pinging nonstop from other women asking me if you're single!

He frowned. Killian's tabloid story on the fire had been posted online before the fire had even been put out and included a blurry photo of Leo falling through the air with Zoe in his arms. The post and picture had "gone viral," which apparently meant it was now spreading around the internet like a plague. He had no intention of blowing Zoe's privacy. He'd lost sight of the dark-haired beauty in the crowd after the fire. But he hadn't been able to get her out of his mind since.

A second text arrived: A woman named Melody Young asked me to pass on her name and number. She's an old friend of your wife. Had lost contact and misses your girls. Wanted to send her condolences and set up a playdate.

The strains on his marriage to Marisa had meant he didn't really know much about her life. While his transfer home to Ottawa had meant the girls had to move to a new house and new school, Theresa had told him the more connections the girls had to their past the more grounded they'd feel.

This is her. Said I'd pass it on to help the girls remember her.

Another text came in before he could answer. It was a picture of a beautiful, blond-haired woman holding a toddler on her lap. He looked closer. The child was Eve.

Leo texted back: Thank you.

No problem, came back the reply. Ready to go over that stuff I uncovered online yet? The story can't stay on ice forever.

No. Leo slid his phone into his pocket without answering. He followed a path and reached a small park. His eyes surveyed the scene. Josh sat on a bench by the water. Alex stood nearby with his back to the street. The location was pretty isolated and yet still close to the road, with good lines of sight. He could only spot two ordinary civilians in the park. One was a well-dressed mother with auburn curls who was pushing a stroller along the riverbank. The other was an older man with a small white puppy, ambling through an outcrop of trees. Neither looked like anyone he'd need to worry about. The tiny ball of puppy fluff started to pull and scrabble on all four paws toward Ivy and Eve. The girls squealed and cooed, and begged Leo to let them go pat it.

But all of that was eclipsed by the site of the petite, dark-haired woman walking toward him. She was dressed simply, in jeans and a tank top that showed off the strength in her arms. Her skin was free of makeup. A simple elastic held back her hair, letting only a few wisps escape and fall around her face. She was even more dazzling than he'd remembered.

"Hey," she said. "How's it going?"

"Not bad," he said. "You?"

"I'm okay." Her dark eyes met his and it was like everything else faded to static around him. There was something about her that hit him like a punch in the gut. An attraction? A feeling? He didn't know what to call it. But it was like someone had attached jumper cables to the dusty remnants of his heart and was trying to jolt it into beating again.

"Daddy!" Eve said. "Can we go see the puppy? Please?"

"It's okay," Zoe said, stepping forward. "I'm happy to watch the girls. I know you and Josh need to talk. We'll stay right around here within eyesight."

Her hand brushed her ear and he saw she was wearing a tiny earpiece. Apparently she'd be staying within earshot, too.

"Please, Daddy? Can we go with her?" Eve's bright eyes brimmed with hope.

"Okay." He hated having the girls beyond arm's length. But he trusted she'd keep them safe, and maybe putting a few feet of distance between himself and Zoe would help keep the jumper-cable jolts at bay. "Zoe, these are my daughters, Ivy and Eve. Girls, this is my friend Zoe. She's really nice and is going to watch you while I talk to my friend Josh. I want you to be very polite and stay where I can see you."

Ivy's skeptical eyes flitted to Zoe's face. Zoe stretched out her hand toward Leo's eldest. "It's very nice to meet you, Ivy."

"I like your bracelet." Ivy eyed her hand.

"Thank you," Zoe said. A tightly woven black-and-green rope encircled her wrist. If she was wearing a microphone, Leo didn't see it. "It's a special kind of rope called a paracord. I wear them all the time. You can unravel it really long and use it for climbing or other useful things. I can show you how to make one."

Ivy paused another moment, then asked, "Do you like dogs?"

"Definitely. I have a terrier at home named Oz. He's very pesky."

"Do you like ice cream?" Eve interjected.

"A bit." Zoe looked at her seriously. "But I prefer sherbet."

Eve's lips scrunched as she pondered this. "Do you like climbing trees?"

"I love climbing." Zoe smiled. "I used to be a gymnast."

"Really?" Eve beamed. "I want to be a gymnast!"

Did she now? Last he'd heard she wanted to be either a princess or a unicorn. But he wasn't exactly surprised. Both girls loved climbing.

Having apparently passed inspection, Zoe started walking with the girls toward the dog.

"I can't climb trees in flip-flops," Eve was saying.

"Well, maybe after we meet the puppy I'll teach you how to climb in bare feet."

Their voices faded to background babble. He let out a long sigh, then turned toward Josh. The former soldier was already on his feet.

"Good to see you." A broad smile crossed Josh's face as he reached out to clasp Leo on the back. "You've met Alex, right?"

"I have." Leo stretched his hand out and shook Alex's hand. "Theresa never told me you were a bodyguard."

A wide grin crossed Alex's face. "We do our best to keep it on the down low. Doesn't always work, but we try. The work we do is one hundred percent confidential."

"I noticed Zoe was wearing an earpiece." Leo looked at Josh. "I take it she can hear our conversation, too?"

"Yep." Josh turned his wrist toward Leo. There was a small microphone implanted in his watch. He had to admit, it was pretty impressive tech.

"I was surprised to hear from you." Leo sat. "I thought you were on your honeymoon."

"I am," Josh said. "But it's the second week and it's hard to keep Samantha off the internet once she knows she's onto something. She found something on The Anemoi's message board we thought you should see." Josh passed Leo his phone. Leo looked down at the picture the waiter had snapped of the vandalized poster of him and the girls. "Did you know that you're The Anemoi's next target?"

FOUR

Leo glanced at the picture of the vandalized poster of his girls, then up to where his girls were now climbing trees with Zoe. The old man with the dog had continued down the path. Eve was hanging upside down from a low tree branch like a koala, while Ivy was halfway up the tree. Leo reached into his wallet, pulled out the first bill he could get his fingers on and pressed it into his old friend's hand. "I'm hiring you, all of you, because I need advice. We can work out the details later. But as of right now, I'm your client and everything we discuss is confidential. Agreed?"

Josh nodded. "Agreed."

Leo let out a long breath. "Yes, I suspected that I was The Anemoi's target. But I didn't know for sure."

Zoe wasn't looking at him but he could see her shoulders flinch, as her earpiece picked up their conversation through Josh's mic. He imagined it bothered her that he hadn't been more forthright with her when they'd swum to safety together after the fire. But open book had never really been his style.

"Does this mean you know what The Anemoi is

trying to steal from you?" Alex asked. "Have they stolen it yet?"

"That's a complicated question with a very complicated answer." Leo turned back to the men. He didn't know how to answer Alex without breaking his cover and spilling classified information. But he trusted they could read between the lines. "I gather Josh told you the story of how we met? It was about six or seven years ago. I was commanding a ship, Josh realized that one member of my crew—a real charmer named Tommy Ferrier—was smuggling some drugs in his bunk. I looked into it, got the proof I needed, and Tommy was discharged and tried. He eventually went home, ruined his life dealing drugs in Canada and went to jail for beating his girlfriend so hard she miscarried. It was an incredibly sad story. But it's why I trust Josh with my life and why I trust you and Zoe by extension."

Josh nodded. So did Alex. Neither answered.

"Now imagine, instead of one ship it was a lot of ships, and instead of one rat on my ship there were a bunch of them scurrying inside a lot of ships, and instead of just telling me that info, Josh had offered to sell it to me for a whole lot of money. After seeing what happened to Tommy Ferrier, I know how important it is that information like that gets handled very carefully and what people would do to keep it from ever coming out. But let's say that my boss just ended up in hospital from a car accident this morning, and I was obligated to get that intel, but I couldn't ask any of my crewmates for help in case they were rats."

"Wow, that would be quite the thing," Alex said.

"Wouldn't it?" asked Leo. Out of the side of his

eye, he saw Zoe flash a smile in his direction. Despite the seriousness of the situation, he felt his shoulders begin to relax. It felt good to know he wasn't alone. "Obviously you can't be involved in my mission, at all. Hands off. If any of you were at an event with me and someone were to approach, you'd all have to ske-daddle and disappear. I can't have outsiders involved in this. You are all civilians with zero clearance. But you can watch my back, keep your eyes open, tell me if you see anything I should be worried about, keep me informed of whatever this Anemoi situation is, and of course make sure my girls aren't touched by any of this."

"Understood," Josh said. "Eyes and ears only. Can I ask what you know about the new, less charitable version of me?"

"The informant?" Leo said. "Not much. He con-tacted my admiral a week ago using robotic-voice-disguising software and an encrypted line. He said he had ample proof of a large-scale rat problem to sell, but that he couldn't trust anyone inside military intelligence to handle the negotiations. The admiral suggested me. I've been overseas for a long time and would spot bad drug-smuggling data in a heartbeat. The informant suggested the exchange happen dur-ing the symposium. I'm authorized to give him a lot of cheese, but only if the intel proves sound."

"Can we assume he's a criminal?" Alex asked.

"Yes and no," Leo said. "He could be selling bad data, or good data, to make money. He could be a whistle-blower who just wants some leverage so he can disappear. You might remember, last year a hacker named Seth Miles found proof that some higher-ups in the military were in the pocket of Eastern European mobsters. He struck a plea deal for espionage, but he's still been branded a pariah and his life was destroyed. It could be someone who doesn't want to repeat what happened to him. Either way, I have to keep his identity a secret. My boss promised him total anonymity, and my work thrives on privacy. So, if all goes smoothly none of you will ever find out who he is." He leaned back on the bench. "That's all I've got for you. Now it's your turn to answer some questions. You're telling me some vigilante group, named The Anemoi, was at the gala last night, attacked Zoe and set the building on fire?"

"Pretty much." Alex nodded.

"And one of them defaced a picture of my girls and posted it online?"

"He used the handle Jason of the Argonauts," Josh said. "He's quite the hacker. When Samantha tried to trace him, he deleted the picture and any trace of himself on the message board."

"My mission, if you want to call it that, is so top secret that nobody knows about it," Leo said. "So only someone very high up could have tipped off The Anemoi to the existence of this intel, or the informant himself did. Both scenarios are bad news. But either way, I don't understand why they'd deface a poster of my daughters."

"We're baffled, too," Josh admitted. "What can we do to help?"

"I've got to go to a bunch of symposium events this week," Leo said, "and hope that the informant approaches me with the intel. I need someone to watch my back and make sure The Anemoi—whoever they are and whatever they want—don't get in the way."

A fresh burst of giggling dragged his attention back to Zoe and the girls. Ivy had dropped to the ground and was lounging in the grass, facing the water. Eve was standing on Zoe's shoulders gripping the thick branch above with both hands. Before he could so much as call out and remind them to be careful, his little girl had scrambled up off Zoe's shoulders and onto the branch.

"How many events are we talking about?" Alex asked.

Leo turned back. "There are symposium meetings tomorrow, a parade on Friday near Toronto and a charity auction back in Ottawa on Saturday, to raise money for children's hospitals. After that the symposium is done and if I don't get the intel by then it's gone."

"Understood," Josh said. "Alex and Zoe have rented rooms at a hotel in Ottawa and can extend their stay a few more days. They can set up the surveillance van in your neighborhood when you're home, make sure the girls are safe and come with you to events. I suggest you don't change anything, act like nothing's wrong and go on with life as usual. Just think of them as extra eyes and ears, watching your back. Nobody ever needs to know you've hired private security."

"Good by me," Leo said. "I'll need someone to take the girls to and from day camp on Thursday. They'll be with me at the parade on Friday."

"All good by me, too," Alex said. Then he called, "Good by you, Zoe?"

Zoe spun back, her dark hair dancing around her shoulders as she flashed two thumbs-up. But as her gaze seemed to linger on Leo's face, for the very first time since they'd met he thought he saw uncertainty in her eyes.

They talked logistics for a few more minutes. Alex would run the surveillance van and be Leo's backup at events. Zoe would take point on security for the girls. Josh was running back to his honeymoon at their Cedar Lake cottage, but he and Samantha would stay in touch. Leo would have the backup he needed, without compromising security. Then Alex went to move the Ash Private Security van from a nearby lot to street parking, so that he could give Leo a tour of it.

Leo stood up, Josh did, too, and for a moment they watched Zoe and the girls. Then Josh slid his hand over his watch, and Leo realized he was covering his microphone.

"Zoe's incredible," Josh said quietly, as if answering a question Leo hadn't asked. "She's battled more criminals and saved more lives than I can begin to count. Alex and I have owed her our lives more than once. I'm guessing you've read the online gossip and know her story?"

"No, I don't," Leo said. He'd come close to it, though. Last night, sitting on his porch in the muggy night air and feeling the memory of her pressing up against the edges of his mind, he'd entered her name in his laptop search engine. But he barely glanced at the first sentence that popped on his screen before shutting it down. He didn't believe in gossip. He didn't want his past to be internet fodder. So why should he treat her the way he wouldn't want to be treated? "I know that she and Alex are stepsiblings. I know that she competed nationally in gymnastics and martial arts.

But that's all I know. I prefer to get to know people in person, not through gossip."

"I'm sure she'll appreciate that," Josh said. "I'll let her tell you her story if and when she's ready. All that really matters to your mission is that she's a bit camera shy and not a fan of media attention. So we're not planning on using her as the inside person for any events right now, let alone by your side. There's too large a risk she'd be identified and the fact the gossip media is determined to find out who the woman in your arms was when you leaped from the burning castle hasn't exactly brought up the best memories for her."

Maybe that was another reason for the distance she'd been keeping and the doubt he'd seen in her eyes. It was probably wise for both of them. She didn't want her name flashed across the tabloids as some damsel in distress he'd plucked from the flames. He wasn't sure he could handle the distraction of having the beautiful bodyguard on his arm, even if they both knew she was only there professionally.

"Hi, Daddy," Eve yelled. "See me?"

"I do." He frowned. His baby girl was now at least six feet off the ground and holding on to the branch with one hand while she waved enthusiastically with the other. While he could usually count on Ivy to be the overprotective older sister, his eldest was now lying contentedly on her stomach watching the small puppy from earlier as it trundled down the path on the other side of the canal.

A black van pulled up on the street. Alex waved out the window. Josh walked up the hill to greet him. Leo started across the grass toward his girls, feeling his brow furrow as he looked at Zoe. The bodyguard met his glance head-on and didn't even flinch.

"Eve, honey." Zoe looked up at the child. "I think your daddy would prefer that you come down and we go find a smaller tree."

His footsteps froze. Zoe had read that in a glance? There'd been something in Zoe's tone—caring, yet firm—that rattled something inside him. There was a spark in Zoe's eyes as she looked up at his daughter, and trust in Eve's eyes as she looked back down at her. Even Ivy was smiling. Whatever this odd pull he'd felt toward Zoe the moment he'd met her, it was almost like his daughters felt a version of it, too.

Help me, Lord, I can't let my mind even begin to think this way. During a particularly rough patch in his marriage to Marisa five years ago, after her first brush with cancer, she'd asked him to promise that when she died he wouldn't bring another woman into their daughters' lives until they were adults. He didn't know why it had mattered so much to her, but it had. That had been around the time her overprotective nature had really kicked into high gear. She'd needed to know he would protect the girls, even if it cost him his heart. He'd promised her that and that pledge to protect their daughters had given them the strength they needed to keep the family together.

He'd never once imagined wanting to break it. Until now.

"But, Zoe—" Eve's lower lip pouted.

"No arguments." Zoe reached her hands up toward the girl. "Come on. We'll find something fun to do down on the ground. Now just turn around on your stomach, slide your legs down to the branch below you and I'll help you down from there."

"It's okay. I'm a lot taller than you are. I'll get her down." He was at least a foot taller than Zoe. He could pluck her out of the tree like a kitten. "Eve! Just stay there and wait for me."

Eve glanced from one adult to the other. Her forehead wrinkled in worry and frustration. "But, I'm almost there."

"Just wait." His voice rose.

Her little voice rose, too. "I want to do it myself!"

Then in one sickening moment everything happened at once. Eve's foothold snapped. Her wail of complaint rose to a scream as she fell. Leo's heart pounded. His little girl tumbled through the air. *Lord, save my baby girl!*

In one fluid moment, Zoe bent her knees, stretched out her arms, and caught the falling child in her arms. Eve hit Zoe in the chest like a tiny, blond cannonball. Zoe absorbed the blow, letting it knock her over as they fell backward into the grass. Zoe lay there in the grass for a moment, her head bent low over Eve's, as she cradled the small girl to her chest.

"You okay, honey?" Zoe asked. Her cheek leaned against Eve's head. Emotion choked in her throat. "That was a very impressive fall."

"The tree broke!" Eve said. His little girl sounded more amazed, even thrilled, than scared or hurt.

The sound that slipped through Zoe's lips was a laugh and a cry in one. Yes, as a parent, he knew that feeling well.

"Yeah, it did," Zoe said softly. "And you were very,

very brave. I've fallen lots and lots of times. You didn't even land on your head like I have!"

The little girl started giggling. Zoe started laughing, too. Then Eve sat up and reached for Leo.

"Daddy, I broke the tree! Zoe caught me." Eve was still giggling.

"I saw that." He knelt down and reached for her.

Zoe half pushed and half lifted Eve up toward her father's waiting arms. "I think your daddy needs a hug right now, too." Zoe's dark eyes searched his face. "My daddy always said it can be a bit scary for a daddy to see their children fall."

Eve's arms slipped around Leo's neck. He lifted her up into a hug, prayers of thanksgiving filling his chest.

"Leo, I'm sorry," Zoe said softly. "My coach used to say that when kids fall it can help them realize just how strong they are."

"A coach isn't a parent." He could tell his voice was sharper than he'd intended. Out of the corner of his eye he was vaguely aware of Ivy moving farther away down the hill, as if she needed distance from his volume. He set Eve down and ran his hand over the back of his neck. "Neither is a bodyguard. If you were a parent, maybe you'd understand that you can't just let kids take risks just because they want to—"

A scream cut off his words, loud and primal, full of fear and indignation.

It was Ivy. "No! Stop! Don't!"

"Ivy! What's wrong?" Leo turned back to where his eldest had been just moments earlier. She was gone. "Where are you?"

Then he saw her pelting toward the water. He ran after her. His arms stretched out toward his eldest, shouting for her to stop. But it was too late. Her small body slipped under the barrier separating the pathway from the quickly flowing canal. She leaned forward, her young form reached out as if she was calling to someone.

Then she plunged into the water.

Agonizing fear pierced Zoe's heart as Ivy's small body was tossed by the current.

"Ivy! Come back!" Leo shouted. His long strides pelted toward the water. Then he vaulted the barrier, plunging into the water after her. Instinctively, Zoe kicked off her own shoes, as well. Then she felt Eve's tiny hand clench hers.

"Daddy won't let Ivy drown, right?" Eve's worried eyes looked up into hers.

Zoe squeezed her hand. "Right."

They held each other tightly, prayers slipping from Zoe's lips as Leo swam for his daughter.

"What happened?" Alex called. She turned. Her brother and Josh were running down the hill toward them.

"I don't know." Tears filled Zoe's eyes. "One moment Leo and I were talking about Eve. The next, Ivy was making a beeline for the water. I think she's trying to swim across the canal."

"Why?" Josh asked.

"I don't know! I looked away for one moment and…"

Her words disappeared into a sob. She was supposed to watch the girls. She'd positioned herself between the girls and the road. It had never even crossed her mind that either girl would suddenly dash toward the water.

"Alex, get downstream and be prepared to help haul them in," Josh said. "Zoe, stay here with Eve and keep her safe. I'm going to call 9-1-1."

Josh ran back to the van. Zoe scooped Eve off the ground and cradled her in her arms. Ivy was still fighting, battling against the current, as she tried to swim across the canal to the opposite shore. Why? Where was she going? What had she seen? Youthful courage and determination filled Ivy's small form, making Zoe's heart ache. She knew that kind of girl. She'd been that kind of girl.

Save her, Lord. Help Leo reach her in time. There's no way she'll be able to make it.

"We can throw the tree branch!" Eve's trusting eyes locked on her face. "It will float. Then Daddy and Ivy can grab it!"

Compassion flooded Zoe's heart. The branch was barely a few inches thick and no help to anyone. *Lord, what do I say?*

"Please, Zoe." Eve's tiny hands grabbed her paracord bracelet. "You told Ivy your bracelet was a rope."

For a fraction of a second all the reasons Eve's idea wouldn't actually work flitted through Zoe's mind, from length, to tensile strength, to range. Then she felt Eve shudder against her shoulder. Eve needed to help. She needed to do something to help get her loved ones out of danger. That was all that mattered.

Ivy went under. For a moment, they lost sight of her. Then she surfaced again.

"Eve, look at me." Zoe turned the small girl's face away from the water. She pulled her bracelet off and slipped it into the girl's hands. "See that van just up the hill? It's got all our supplies in it. We're going to run there as fast as we can and find something to help your daddy and Ivy. You're going to help by unraveling my bracelet for me, okay?"

Eve nodded, tears shining on her pale face. Zoe ran for the van, clutching Eve to her chest. Even from yards down the hill, she could see Josh standing by its open door, the phone to his ear, talking to emergency services.

Lord, what do I have? We don't have life jackets or life preservers. I don't even know what we have that floats besides the storage containers.

"Josh!" Zoe shouted. "Toss me a round storage lid!"

He didn't even pause. Shoving the phone into the crook of his neck, Josh reached into the van, yanked the thick, plastic lid off the closest storage container and threw it at her like a Frisbee. The plastic lid soared down the hill. Zoe shifted Eve to one arm, reached up and plucked it from the air.

"Okay, Eve, we've got something we can throw," Zoe said. The thought of taking Eve up the hill to Josh's care filled her mind, but Eve clutched Zoe so tightly around the neck she could barely breathe. She didn't have time to climb up the hill to the van. She didn't have time to argue with Eve. Eve was coming with her. She swung the small child around onto her back until she was piggyback. "You hold on very tight, okay?"

"Okay." Eve's small arms wrapped around her.

Zoe sprinted down that path to where Alex stood, anxious and ashen, watching Leo battle the current to reach his child. Ivy had given up trying to cross and was now trying to swim back, but the current kept pushing her farther downstream.

Panic washed over Ivy's face. Her limbs churned desperately in the water.

"Daddy! Help me!" Ivy screamed.

The water swept over her head. Leo's daughter went under.

FIVE

Zoe watched as Leo's eyes locked firm on his drowning child. He swam for Ivy, forcing his body through the water toward her.

"Ivy!" he shouted. "Hang on!"

She struggled back to the surface, gulping for breath. "Daddy!"

"Don't worry. I'm coming!" Leo's face shone with a determination and protective love that made something knock inside Zoe's chest. Ivy went under again. Leo dove for her. His arms locked around Ivy. She looped her frail arms around his neck, looking small against her father's broad chest. He held her with one arm and kicked toward shore. Water streamed down his face. Prayers of relief poured from his lips. Pulling the cord from Eve's hands, Zoe tied it quickly around the lid handle.

"Alex!" she shouted.

Her brother looked up. She sent the lid flying down the path toward him. Alex leaped for it and caught it, the lid barely seeming to touch his hand before he sent it flying out over the water. Leo grabbed it and pushed it under Ivy like a flutter board. The cord went tight in Alex's hands and for a moment she thought it was about to snap. Then Alex looped it around his hand and leaned back, pulling Leo and Ivy in.

"See, Eve?" Zoe said. "They're going to be okay. I'm going to help Ivy get back over the railing, okay? But I need to set you down first."

Eve slithered from her back. Zoe ran for the railing. Ivy was babbling incoherently, trying to talk, even as she gasped for breath. Zoe reached through the railing, grabbed Ivy's hand and helped her through. Ivy's feet hit dry land. Zoe dropped to her knees and let the frightened, waterlogged girl tumble into her arms. Zoe held her tightly, tears filling her eyes as she felt Ivy shudder against her. Then she felt the weight of Eve's body slamming against her, too, and she pulled the smaller girl into the hug as well, wrapping her arms around both sisters as the girls cried, hugged each other.

"Thank you," Leo said.

She looked up over the girls' heads and watched as Leo dragged his body over the railing and collapsed on the pavement, looking both so strong and so weak she felt something wrench inside her heart. Then Leo reached out his arms, whispered his daughters' names, and Zoe let the girls go as they flew into their father's arms.

"Well done," Alex said softly. Her brother reached down for her hand. She let him pull her to her feet. It had been moments, barely minutes, since Ivy's body had hit the water yet the time had seemed to stretch to hours.

Leo was still kneeling down on the path, his arms around his daughters.

"I'm sorry... I didn't know... I was trying to help the dog...but the water..." Ivy babbled, struggling to get words out as they choked and caught in her throat.

"It's okay." Leo shushed her. His hand ran over the back of her head. "It doesn't matter. All that matters is you're okay."

"It does matter!" Ivy's voice rose. She pressed her hands against Leo's chest and shoved him back. "Listen! Please! I was trying to save him! A bad man tried to kill the puppy!"

Ivy continued to push back against him until he let her go. Her shaking arm stretched out pointing desperately farther down the canal toward the small rock outcropping under the bridge. "The fluffy white one we patted. The man tried to drown him. I was watching. When you were all paying attention to Eve, he looked right at me, lifted the dog and dropped him in the water." Tears of panic and fear coursed from her eyes. "On purpose! When he knew I was watching him! He threw him in the water on purpose."

Leo was still shaking his head, like he wasn't sure what to think or what to believe. "You jumped in the river and nearly drowned trying to save a dog?"

Ivy nodded. Her eyes filled with the desperate, panicked tears of someone still so young, yet so close to the cusp between childhood and adolescence. "He threw him in."

"And you tried to save it yourself without calling to me for help?" Leo asked.

Ivy looked down at the pavement. Sirens roared in the distance.

"Ivy, I believe you." Zoe knelt down in front of the small family. "But right now you need to take your dad and your sister up to the van, and get dried off, and talk to the police when they get here. Josh has some nice, big towels in the van. I'm going to try and find the puppy."

"Promise?" Ivy and Eve seemed to speak at once. Two sets of children's eyes were locked on her face.

"I promise to try." Zoe stood up. "But you have to go up to the van right now, and listen to your dad, and do what he says."

She turned and started down the path in the direction Ivy had pointed. She heard Leo and his daughters heading up the hill behind her. Then she felt her brother's hand brush her shoulder.

"Zoe," Alex said.

"Don't start," she said. Her eyes searched the water for any glimpse of life. "Those two little girls have been traumatized enough for one day. I'm going to find the dog."

"You can't—"

"Don't you dare tell me I can't find it!" Zoe said. "Someone cruel and evil tried to drown a dog to scare two little girls. He did it after making sure the girls had bonded with it, which means he's trying to send a message. Which means, he dropped the dog somewhere it can be found."

"I know," Alex said softly. His steps paced hers as they searched the water. "I was going to say, you can't blame yourself for this. This isn't your fault. Her father was right there with you, too. Neither of you had any reason to believe she'd leap in the water. The exact same thing could've happened to either me or Josh—"

"There!" Then she saw it—a tiny, miserable bundle of white fur clinging to an outcrop of rocks. *Thank*

You, God! The dog was still alive. She pulled out her earpiece and pressed both it and her cell phone into her brother's hand. Then she leaped up onto the railing. "Tell me you'll keep that makeshift floatation device handy."

"Of course."

Zoe dove neatly into the river. Instantly the current wrapped around her, yanking hard against her body. She gritted her teeth and swam for the frightened animal. Water beat against her body. Underwater rocks scraped and battered against her legs. She made it to the outcropping, braced her legs and reached her hand out toward the puppy.

"Come on, dog." She stretched her fingers out as far as she could, coaxing the animal toward her. "Come here. I've got you."

The puppy scrambled into the crook of her arms and licked her face furiously. A chuckle slipped her lips. She pressed the dog against her chest. "It's okay," she whispered. Her fingers looped through the dog's collar. "I've got you. You're okay."

Lord, what kind of monster would throw a puppy in the water? How do I protect Leo's daughters from them?

Something cold and plastic brushed against her fingers. There was a small bag wedged under the dog's collar, tied to it by a small zip tie. She eased it out. There was a tiny envelope inside it.

Leo sat with one long leg in and one leg out of the Ash Private Security van. His girls leaned over him and told their rambling stories to a couple of officers. The police looked a bit lost. To be honest, Leo couldn't blame them. Three police cars and an ambulance had converged on-site responding to a 9-1-1 call about a drowning child. Instead, they'd found nobody drowning and two small girls babbling about someone throwing a dog in the river. Emergency lights still flashed around them. Two paramedics had rushed down to the water, presumably in case Zoe and Alex, who were still down there, needed help. Not that he knew of any reason why the siblings would need help, but he couldn't see them from the van. Emergency vehicles were lined up along the road and regular traffic was slowing down to see what the commotion was about. He could hear the whir of rotors overhead now, but couldn't tell if they were from a rescue helicopter or a news one.

"Do you want to file a report, sir?" The question came from a tall officer with a bushy moustache standing to Leo's right. All of the emergency service people who'd arrived on the scene were being nothing but exceedingly professional, efficient and polite. But it didn't stop Leo from suspecting they thought their time might have been wasted.

"You want to file a report," Ivy said. "Right, Daddy?"

He looked down. Both girls' gazes were locked seriously on his face.

Guide me, please, God. I don't know what to think right now.

The vandalized poster of the girls flashed before his mind's eye. The Anemoi had set the castle on fire and defaced a picture of his daughters. Now his daughter claimed someone had thrown a puppy into the water, right in front of her. The idea those three things could be linked somehow was pretty far-fetched. But the thought of them just being a coincidence didn't ring much better.

If the old man had thrown the dog into the water on purpose, he'd have had absolutely no way of knowing that Ivy would jump into the water after it. The thought that some stranger had intentionally lured Ivy into the water was a pretty big stretch.

So then what would his motivation for drowning a puppy be? To scare Leo's daughters? To upset them?

"You do believe me, right, Daddy?" Ivy asked.

"Sweetie, I want to believe you," he said. "But what you said about the man and the puppy doesn't make sense. And I don't understand why you didn't ask me for help instead of running off like that and trying to fix it all by yourself. I'm just very, very thankful you're okay."

He slid his arm around her. But her small shoulders stiffened like a board, like his daughter's mind and heart were locked deep inside her again, somewhere he couldn't reach them.

"Excuse me! Coming through!" Zoe's voice rang out strong and clear above the din. "I said, 'Excuse me.'"

He watched as she pushed through the crowd, politely but firmly nudging officers twice her size out of her way, as she ran toward the van. Then she reached them. Her hands stretched out, past him, toward the girls.

"There's someone who wants to see you," she said. She pushed a small, wet, squirming bundle of puppy into Ivy's outstretched arms.

A soft, whimper-like squeal slipped through Ivy's lips. She buried her face in the dog's fur and for the first time Leo realized just how sick with worry his daughters had probably been. Ivy looked up at Zoe with tear-filled eyes. "You rescued him!"

"Of course I did," Zoe said softly. "I promised you I would try."

Tears began to slip down Ivy's cheeks, Eve launched herself into her sister's arms, and for a long moment he watched the small, hugging bundle of girls and puppy, feeling a lump of emotion sit heavily in the back of his throat.

He heard Zoe thank God under her breath. He turned and faced her. Her body was muddy and soaked. Tears brimmed in the corners of her huge, dark and luminescent eyes. For a moment, it took all the self-control in his chest not to reach out, sweep his arms around her and pull her into the van to join in the family embrace.

Instead, he got out of the van and stood.

"Thank you," he said.

"No problem," she said. "We need to talk, privately, without an audience."

"Understood." He took a few moments to make sure the police had all they needed from him, that the girls were happily occupied with the puppy, and that Josh and Alex had a close, watchful eye on his family. Then Leo and Zoe walked to a nearby bench. He sat, sideways, close enough that he could see both girls but far enough away that they couldn't hear his words. Then he turned back to Zoe. "Go ahead."

"When were you going to tell me that you were a spy?" she asked.

"I'm not a spy."

Zoe crossed her arms. "You can trust me, you know."

"I know and I'm not a spy," he repeated, slower this

time and with added emphasis. "I am a naval commander with security clearance and a great deal of battle experience in certain types of operations."

And a mission to get smuggling intel from an informant.

"Do you really think the military has another Seth Miles situation on its hands?" she asked. "A mole who's trying to stop crime and see justice happen?"

"You mean could our informant be a good guy? Or someone who has good intentions? I don't know. I hope so. I pray for them." He ran both hands through his hair. "I pray for this whole entire mess."

"I need to show you something." She pulled a small laminated card from her pocket and pressed it into his hands. "There was an envelope on the dog's collar. It's addressed to you."

He pulled out a simple plain white card. It was blank except for the scrawled picture of a crude black storm cloud. Forks of lightning shot from its depths.

"We've seen this symbol before on The Anemoi message boards," Zoe said. "It's like their calling card."

"So these criminals have gone from setting fire to a castle full of people to terrorizing my children?"

It took all the self-control he had not to crumple the page in anger and disgust. Instead, he dropped his head into his hands. This was all about retrieving smuggling secrets from an informant, wasn't it? How did scaring his children fit into that? *What am I missing? What am I not seeing?*

Then he felt Zoe's hand brush his back and for a moment let himself take comfort in the simple touch of her hand. "Maybe they're warning you not to go after the intel. Or they're warning you what will happen if you do."

He sat up again, pulling his shoulder away from her.

"This isn't a warning," he said. "It's a taunt. A warning is specific. So is a demand. I learned, time and again in my very long career, that whether you're going against ships, groups or individuals with evil in their hearts, that you need to take warnings seriously. But taunts? Taunts are somebody else's garbage way to provoke you into doing something you don't want to do. You were an athlete. Weren't you ever taunted?"

"Yes," she said slowly, "I know what it's like to be taunted."

"And did you ever do anything you regretted because of it?" he asked.

"Yes." Her one-word answer cut like an unexpected chill through the air. Then, to his surprise, her slim shoulders rose and fell, like she was watching a particularly unhappy memory play through her mind. For a moment he felt the impulse to give her a hug and ask what the memory was that upset her so much. Instead he crossed his arms in front of his chest.

"Well, I can't afford to let some ragtag group of vigilantes taunt me or distract me from getting this intel," he said. "I remember I used to see ratty old pirate boats pull up alongside the beautiful, powerful battleship I was commanding, and have to order my crew not to respond when their sailors lined the decks taunting us with lewd gestures and obscenities. Because I never knew if it was a trap or what could happen if we got goaded into a fight. Not to mention how many times I had to discipline somebody under my command for getting into a fistfight because somebody insulted their honor. I don't know why they're taunting me, or what they're trying to provoke me to do. But it's not going to work. I can't let it. There's too much counting on me."

"But your daughter..." Zoe started.

"My daughter should've asked us for help instead of trying to settle matters by herself." He stood, wishing not for the first time that his eldest hadn't turned out quite so much like himself. "The Anemoi had no way of knowing she'd do that. But it doesn't change the fact that protecting the girls has to be my top priority. Now even more than ever."

He strode back toward the van. The sooner he met the informant, got the intel and analyzed it, the sooner this would all be over and his daughters would be safe. Alex and Josh were standing sentry by the door in an incredibly casual way that made it look like they were just two buddies killing time. His girls were huddled happily on the van floor playing with the puppy now. He could sense Zoe walking behind him, as if all the questions moving through her mind were slipping out as whispers in the air. He knew she wanted him to sit back down and talk with her, like they were friends or the kind of people who solved their problems together.

But he had to take his children home, get them changed into clean clothes and remind them of the importance of telling him if they saw anything that upset or worried them. He had to review his symposium schedule for tomorrow and figure out which sessions he'd be sitting through as apparently his mission wasn't over so his cover still needed to be upheld. He had to put in a call to the local animal shelters and police station about the dog his daughters had inexplica-

bly named Fluff on the very slim possibility someone
stepped forward to claim it, not to mention go buy all
the necessary pet supplies on the very likely instance
that nobody did and so the dog was now theirs.

He had a whole list of things to do, most important
of all was putting distance between himself and that
beautiful woman who, yet again, challenged him and
drew him in at the same time. Of all the battles he
was fighting, on all sides, one of the largest was the
flicker of something that Zoe threatened to awake in
his heart. He couldn't let that happen.

After Josh left to go back to his honeymoon at
Cedar Lake, Alex and Zoe followed Leo's truck in
the black nondescript Ash Security van. They waited
in the parking lot while he and the girls went into a pet
store and practically loaded his truck full of every toy
and piece of dog gear Ivy and Eve imagined the dog
they had named Fluff might want. Then they waited
again while he went into the grocery store and loaded
up on groceries, before finally going home. The girls
waved the van good-night and he took them inside. Pe-
riodically in the evening he'd look out and see it there,
just calmly parked somewhere on the street or pulling
smoothly through the neighborhood.

After the girls had gone to bed, he sat with his coffee on the front porch, listened to the wind in the trees
and the roar of the Ottawa River in the distance, and
stared through the foliage at the dark tinted windows.
Was it Zoe inside or Alex? He didn't know. Nor why
it had felt so odd somehow to run those errands and
then make a meal without going out and inviting them
in. He'd hired them to watch his back. Nothing more.
And yet, he found himself walking into the kitchen,

pulling a second coffee cup out of the cupboard and looking at it. What would happen if he poured a second coffee, walked outside and knocked on the van? What if Zoe was there and he invited her to join him on the porch? There was nothing wrong with grabbing a coffee with your private security to go over planning details. Surely, if he called and gave her a heads-up, they'd find a way to arrange a conversation without blowing her cover. Not to mention, he had several friends who were female—Alex's fiancée, Theresa, was one of them—who he wouldn't think twice about having coffee with.

But somehow this was different, as if the simple act of pouring Zoe a coffee and knocking on a door would open himself up to something more and tempt his damaged heart into wanting something he couldn't have. He put the mug back in the cupboard, turned off the lights and lay on his couch, staring at the ceiling and trying to pray. But instead, he found himself lost in the memory of a pair of dark, luminous eyes.

Zoe was waiting for him in the driveway the next morning, standing by the driver's side door of his red pickup truck, in blue jean leggings and a long gray T-shirt. Despite the fact he'd practically had to drag his girls to get dressed and out the door, the moment they laid eyes on Zoe they squealed, leaped off the porch and ran across the lawn to her. Eve launched herself into Zoe's arms for a hug. Then, to his surprise, Ivy gave her a super fast hug, too.

"Daddy's making us leave Fluff at home!" Ivy said petulantly.

"Well, that sounds very smart of your daddy," Zoe

said seriously. "Dogs don't like summer day camp. I'm sure Fluff will be very happy to help guard the house."

That seemed to settle the matter and the girls climbed in the backseat of the truck. What? He'd gone six rounds with the girls earlier about making Fluff stay at home, but they'd been willing to accept it from Zoe without so much as a squeak? It was something in her voice. Something that made her sound like she was on your side but that things just had to go another way. It made a person want to follow her.

"Morning, Leo! So, you'll be going in the van with Alex and I'll be driving your truck." She stretched out her hand, ready to catch his keys.

"I'll drive my truck," he said, "and drop you off."

"But then you'll have to drive all the way out to Nepean just to turn around and go back downtown." Zoe's arms crossed. "It makes a lot more sense for me to drive your truck and you to catch a ride with Alex. I'd offer to take them in my car, but Alex and I drove out to Ottawa together in the van. I promise you, I'm a very good driver. I only crash when people are shooting at me." A smile turned at the corner of her lips. It was quirky and playful, and made him even more grateful he hadn't given in and asked her to join him for coffee last night.

He felt his brow furrow. "I'll drive."

He didn't talk on the way to day camp. He didn't need to. Eve chirped away from the backseat, telling Zoe all about Fluff's first big night in the house and asking her questions all about her dog back home. Even Ivy joined in, here and there, which was a change from her usual habit of staring out the window. He dropped them off at a beautiful, old-fashioned one-room schoolhouse, where the Department of Defence was holding day camp for children from military and government families.

There were government security personnel on-site and a whole fleet of diplomatic cars waiting in case something arose and Zoe needed to leave with the girls. Still, he stressed that he'd return to pick them up personally. As he eased the truck back down the highway into the downtown core, he wondered what Zoe would do all day, while she waited for the girls. Would she grab a coffee and sit in a lobby to wait? Would she volunteer to join in the crafts, making things out of macaroni and glue?

He gave Alex a quick call and told him he could take the day off, go back to the hotel to get some sleep in an actual bed, before another long stint in the surveillance van. Leo's day would be spent with symposium delegates, in lectures as people talked about their various roles and work in different places around the world. They were fascinating stories, truth be told, but still the time seemed to crawl as Leo's eyes drew him back to the clock on the wall.

Zoe and the girls were waiting for him on the schoolhouse yard practicing handstands. The girls tumbled into the truck, faces flushed and eyes aglow.

"Daddy!" Eve bounced up and down on her seat. "Zoe taught the class how to fight!"

"Did she, now?" His eyebrows rose.

"I volunteered to help out," Zoe said. "They did sports in the afternoon and so I showed them some combat moves. Basic stuff."

"Can Zoe stay for dinner?" Ivy asked. "She said she likes pizza."

Two sets of hopeful eyes stared up at him through the rearview mirror. An unsettled feeling brushed the back of his neck. The girls were quickly becoming attached to Zoe.

"We'll see," he said. "I'm sure Zoe's very busy."

Just like that the light in the girls' eyes fell. He pulled out of the parking lot and started for the highway. He was now the bad guy in his daughters' eyes again because he wasn't about to welcome a stranger into their home? Not that Zoe was typical. She had rescued a puppy, caught Eve when she fell from a tree and showed them fighting moves. It was no wonder they were crazy about her.

"Leo?" Zoe said softly. She leaned toward him. Her hand brushed his arm. He pulled away, startled by the sudden contact. But the next words from her mouth wiped any worry she was being affectionate from his mind. "We're being followed."

SIX

His eyes rose to the rearview mirror. A black sedan with diplomatic plates was following close behind them. He pulled smoothly through a parking lot and onto a side street. The sedan shot past, and for a moment he thought he'd lost it. But in seconds, the car was behind him again. Leo turned to Zoe. "You're right."

He leaned forward and hit the stereo. Instantly, happy, bopping children's music filled the cab. He adjusted the speakers so the music came out the back.

"So, what do we do?" Zoe asked softly.

He pulled onto the highway and chose the middle lane. The black sedan matched pace.

"We do nothing. I can't outrun a vehicle in a high-speed chase with my daughters in the car. The vehicle has diplomatic plates. Anyone from the symposium could've borrowed it from the pool. They're not about to open fire on a crowded highway. We ignore them, pretend we don't know they're there and let them follow." Zoe shook her head. She pulled her cell phone from her pocket. Before she could dial, his hand landed on hers. "Don't! If you call the police the girls will hear the call."

"I'm not." She pulled her hand away, raised her phone and took a picture of the car. "I'm texting a picture of the car and the license plate to Alex. He can call the police. They can be on the lookout for it. He can also run the plates, although if you're right it'll just take us back to the symposium."

He held the steering wheel firmly at ten and two and prayed under his breath as the car closed the gap between them. It was following too close. The driver's face was hidden in the black hood of a sweatshirt. Traffic hemmed around them. The car nudged closer still until its bumper almost brushed against Leo's truck. Zoe's hand tightened on the door handle. *Help me, Lord, I don't want to risk an accident with the girls in the car. But if I try to shake him, I might endanger my daughters' lives.* He waited for a gap in traffic and then pulled into the right-hand lane. An exit loomed ahead. He hit his signal and shifted as late as he dared. Horns sounded and tires shrieked as the black car swerved across traffic to follow him.

But Leo was almost home. Just three more blocks and he'd be on his street, leading the driver directly to his house. He couldn't let that happen. There was a family pizza parlor ahead on his left. He pulled neatly into the parking lot. Leo's eyes cut to the rearview mirror just in time to see the black car speed past. The car's window rolled down. An empty soft drink cup flew from the window and clattered to the ground just inches away from his truck. Then the car disappeared down the street.

"Surprise, girls," he said. "We're getting pizza for dinner."

A cheer went up from the backseat. He cut the engine and turned to Zoe. "Sorry for the change of plans, but I thought it would be a good idea to be somewhere public. I'm going to go in and get a table for me and the girls. Can you call Alex to meet us here?"

Zoe opened her mouth, but no words came out. He didn't wait. Leo walked his girls into the pizza place, got them a table by the window and set them up with coloring pages. Outside he could see Zoe pacing the parking lot, hands in the air like she was battling an invisible foe. Moments later the Ash van pulled into the lot. After a quick glance from Zoe, Alex walked into the restaurant.

"Hey, man," Alex said. "Mind if I sit down and join the girls? I think Zoe wants to talk to you, and I'm an expert at coloring."

Leo walked out to the parking lot. Zoe made a beeline for him.

"We got another taunt." She held up the cup. His eyes glanced down at the familiar shape of a menacing storm cloud. "Someone followed your truck down the highway and threw an empty cup out the window with a storm cloud drawn on it."

"I see." His arms crossed. "I'm sure Alex will run the plates and see if it's possible to narrow down who took the vehicle out."

"I don't understand how you can be so calm about this!" Zoe said. "Talking to you is like trying to chip away slowly at a big, thick block of ice. Do you have human emotions? I don't know about you, but I'm furious that someone would do this to those two amazing little girls. First terrifying them at the park yesterday and now this!"

She wiped her hand across the air as if mapping out where his invisible ice wall would be.

"What should I have done? Endangered and frightened my children by getting into a wild car chase?" He grabbed her hand out of thin air and held it. Who was she to tell him he didn't have emotions? Just because he preferred to keep his to himself while she broadcast hers like a megaphone. "Don't you get it? They're trying to intimidate me. They're trying to scare me. And I don't scare easily."

Protective anger was practically radiating from Zoe's body. But he knew it wasn't directed at him. Instead, the fury that anyone would hurt his children was what flashed like lightning in her eyes. "But your daughters—"

"Will be in even more danger if I don't control my emotions," he interrupted. "You said yesterday that you'd been taunted by bullies before. Did they ever cause you to lose your temper? Did you ever lash out and do something you regretted?"

She pulled her hand out of his grasp and crossed her arms in front of her chest. "You know the answer to that question. It's the first thing that probably came up when you looked me up online before hiring me. You know I elbowed a guy in the face on national television."

"No, I didn't know that, actually," he said. "Because I didn't look you up. Because I trusted you and your past is immaterial to me. We all did foolish things we regretted when we were younger. But we're adults now, with kids to protect. You're not a parent. I know not everyone thinks like a parent and some people aren't even cut out to be parents, but all that matters right now is protecting those girls and getting that data from the informant. The informant didn't approach me today. But hopefully he will tomorrow. Then I'll get the data, process it, pass it on to Admiral Jacobs when he gets out of hospital or to someone else the data tells me is clean. The Anemoi might be trying to get their hands on the same data that I am, but they won't succeed. The sooner I get the intel, the sooner this will all be over with and my daughters will be safe again."

"But what if you're wrong?" Zoe's face had gone white. She shook her head so furiously her hair danced around her head. "I told you that The Anemoi are vigilantes. They ruin lives. They utterly destroy them. If they're targeting you—if they're taunting you— then there's something you have that somebody wants, or something terrible that somebody thinks you've done. You need to let Samantha do a complete sweep of your past. Of anyone you've wronged. Of anyone you've hurt, starting with that Tommy Ferrier guy you got thrown into jail for drug smuggling. Because if I'm right, this won't be over when you get that data and pass it up the chain. This will be over when The Anemoi gets what it wants."

"I told you, I don't have anything to steal."

"Then what about Marisa?" Zoe said. "Could she have done something? Did she rack up heavy debts that you weren't aware of? Were there people she brought into the girls' lives or associated with that were trouble? Did she gamble? Did she shoplift? Did she do illegal drugs? Or see other men?"

"Stop!" He held up his hand. "I know you're trying to help. But you didn't know Marisa. She was deeply devoted to Ivy and Eve. She was overprotective, bordering on paranoid. She would never allow anything in her life that would hurt our daughters. So much so that after her first diagnosis with cancer, she made me promise that if anything ever happened to her I wouldn't even bring another woman into the girls' lives or consider remarrying until they were adults."

"I don't get it." The words flew from Zoe's mouth in a rush. "How does depriving your daughters of ever having a stepmom make Marisa a good mother?"

Leo stepped back. Pain filled his chest as sharply as if she'd just punched him. How dare she judge Marisa like that? First Marisa's life had been knocked sideways by an unexpected teenage pregnancy and then she'd been left to raise two daughters practically solo while Leo had been overseas. She'd had the right to be overprotective and worry that Leo might make another mistake and bring the wrong woman into their lives. Hadn't she?

And if not, he'd agreed to it. He couldn't go back on his word now.

Zoe stepped back, too, her eyes on his face as if reading the pain in his silence. "I'm sorry. That was out of line. I didn't mean to imply..."

Her words trailed off. But maybe it was better she didn't finish the sentence.

"It's okay," he said. "I'm happy to just pretend you didn't say that and move on. But the one thing you need to know about Marisa, rightly or wrongly, is that she protected the girls before all else."

Silence spread out between them again. Zoe looked down at the ground. He couldn't tell if he was upset at her question or The Anemoi, or this entire situation.

"Look," he added. "You've had a really long day.

How about you go back to your hotel and relax for a bit. I don't need you watching my back to have dinner with my girls."

She nodded, but didn't say a word. Somehow her silence unnerved him more than her talking.

"As you know, tomorrow's the parade," he went on, "and because it's near Toronto, Theresa will be able to be there. The girls love her. She's been a wonderful therapist to them. I'm going to request that Alex and Theresa accompany me on the float with the girls. Then Saturday, I'll get a second ticket for Alex to accompany me to the auction. I'm sure Nigel won't mind, especially since I got dinner at a five-star restaurant and front row theater tickets to auction off."

Another nod. She still wasn't arguing. She wasn't saying anything.

"Josh has invited the girls and me up to Cedar Lake once the symposium is done," he added. "I'll talk through your suspicions with them that this might be personally motivated, and see what we come up with. Marisa did have a laptop and she did keep an electronic diary. But I deleted it when she died. I just couldn't bear to read it. Maybe Samantha can retrieve it. Again, I'm still hoping that once my informant makes contact and I get the data that this will all be over."

"So are you going to walk in there and tell my brother that you're sidelining me for the rest of the week, and want him to have your back?" she asked. "Or do you want me to do it? Because, I'm warning you, he's very protective."

Why did this infuriating woman always have to be so direct? She might have said talking to him was like trying to chip through ice, but talking to her was like getting pelted with fireballs and being expected to expertly volley them back.

"I had the impression from Josh that you didn't like the spotlight," he said. "Do you really want to be stuck with us on some parade float waving to the crowd or escorting me around some fancy ballroom?"

"I just don't want to be sidelined." Her hands snapped to her hips. "Obviously, Alex and I will talk things out, plan and come up with the best possible way to watch your back and protect your daughters. And if you want Alex on the float that's what will happen. But I'm good at what I do. I care about protecting you and those girls. I don't want you ignoring me and pushing me into the shadows."

Ignoring her? He was trying to keep from being hung up on her, even fixated on her. She was like some magnetic field pulling his attention to her. Didn't she feel it? Was she really going to make him come out and say it?

"I know you're good at what you do," he said, "but I have to think about what's best for my children."

"You don't trust me to protect them." She said it like it wasn't even a question.

Why didn't she understand? The problem was with him, not her. He was the one battling an attraction like he'd never felt before, one that had the potential of hurting his children as well as breaking the promise he'd made to his wife.

"Today, we were pursued by a vehicle down the highway and we had different approaches on how to handle it," he said. "If you had been driving things could've turned out very differently."

"I know how to drive in dangerous situations," Zoe

said. "I would've told them what was going on, told them to get low and got them home safely. I would have never put them in danger."

"It's not just today," he said. "Yesterday Ivy managed to run and jump into the water while we were both watching her. I still haven't managed to get her to open up about that or explain why she tried to rescue Fluff all by herself instead of telling me what was happening and asking for help. It's like she's shut me out from whatever's going on in her mind."

"Did you try listening to her?" Zoe asked.

"I can't listen to her if she won't talk to me."

She sighed. "Maybe you should try listening to the words she's not saying."

He blinked. It was the kind of thing Marisa would say and he had no idea what she meant by it. But he recognized all too well the look she was giving him. It was the same look of disbelief and frustration he'd seen in Marisa's eyes every time she thought he was missing the obvious. As if the women in his life, including his daughters, had their own secret language, which he'd never learned and was somehow blamed for not knowing. Something about it hit him like a cold, wet towel to the face. Maybe the pull he felt toward Zoe was one-sided. Maybe it was all in his mind, but not in hers, and just like Marisa she was unwilling to receive or return what he offered her.

"I appreciate that you're trying to help," he said. "But I have to think about what's best for my girls."

No matter how much something inside him wanted her there, by his side, in his arms and as part of his sad and broken little family.

Zoe clenched her jaw so tightly it quivered. "Got it, Boss."

For a long moment they stood there, eyes locked on each other, neither one willing to break their gaze. Then she turned and walked back to the van.

It was quarter after eleven in the morning, and the Ontario town was packed with people who'd driven in for the parade and street festival. Zoe sat on a stool at a small high table in the front of a café. The sliding front window had been opened all the way creating an open patio feel and giving her the perfect vantage point. A text from Samantha this morning had confirmed that a member of The Anemoi who went by Dionysus took credit for dropping Fluff in the river, but there was no word about further actions against Leo or the parade.

"Man, this shindig is taking its time to start." Alex's voice echoed in her earpiece. "Theresa, the girls and I are all good. We're standing at the front of the float. How's the view from the sky, Leo?"

Zoe raised her bracelet microphone to her mouth, using her cell phone as cover. "The sky?"

"The Canadian delegation float was built around a cherry picker." Leo's voice took over the airwaves. "Alex, Theresa and the girls are standing on the truck bed. We decided the girls would be safest there. I'm up in the hydraulic bucket."

"There's a decorative arch spanning the road, near the end of the route, just before we turn the corner." Alex chuckled. "Our driver says we should clear it no problem. I mean, really it'll be fine. But you should've seen the look on Leo's face when he told him that he should be prepared to duck just in case."

Alex was still laughing as the line went quiet again.

She leaned her elbows on the table and tried to settle the jitters hearing Leo's voice had caused. When she'd first started with Ash Private Security, it had been hard enough hearing her own brother and Josh in her head, and she'd known them almost all her life. Having Leo's deep, baritone growl suddenly whispering in her ear was a whole other experience.

"Alrighty." Alex's voice was back. "We're getting ready to move. The floats are going to park in the side street behind the fairgrounds. We'll meet you there afterward and walk over to the fair together, so Leo and the girls can spend some time in the Canadian heroes booth."

None of this was news, but Alex was a big fan of running commentaries on missions like these. Thankfully, the police, military, firefighters and paramedics fair booths were all clumped together in a semicircle and Samantha had already managed to wrangle a list of who'd be manning them and run them through a background check. Everyone had checked out. All they had to do was get Leo and the girls through the parade and they'd be home free. The street was a different matter. As crowded as the café was around her, it was nothing compared to the street below her. Parents, children and grandchildren lined the sidewalk, huddled on laps and sitting on small fold-out chairs and blankets. Families were everywhere.

You're not a parent. Leo's words echoed in her mind. *Maybe if you were a parent you'd understand.*

It was like he'd kept hammering that point home,

both in the park and in the parking lot, oblivious to how his words stabbed her in the heart. Growing up, she'd never really wanted children. Maybe it was because she hadn't had a mother or a sibling until her dad married Alex's mom. Or maybe it was just because she'd been a tomboy and never into dolls. But in the terrible weeks and months that followed her suspension from the national gymnastic team after she'd elbowed Killian Lynch in the face on live television, her stepmom had been so worried for her health, she'd gently urged her to see a doctor. Her parents had wondered if she had depression. But instead the routine appointment had led to questions about hormone levels, which had in turn led to unexpected blood tests, then scans and finally the verdict, when she was just sixteen, that she was unlikely to ever have children of her own.

She'd felt like it was all her fault.

Of course her doctor and family had assured that it wasn't. But something inside her stubborn, sixteen-year-old heart had felt like somehow in the split second it had taken to lose her temper and swing an elbow back at the taunting creep behind her, she'd disqualified herself from parenthood just like she'd disqualified herself from competing. "Some people just aren't cut out to be parents" was one of those lines people like Leo would say. That was how she felt, just not cut out, like some faulty paper doll left behind on the page.

A cheer echoed down from the end of the street. A large Canadian flag appeared on the horizon followed by men and women in uniform, marching in unison, waving to the crowd, throwing out what she knew from the intel would be maple candy. Then she saw the naval float and nearly laughed into her tea. It was a giant, cardboard and papier-mâché battleship, bedecked in flags, moving at a snail's crawl. She watched its slow approach. Eve and Ivy stood on the bow flanked by Theresa and Alex on either side. Eve was bouncing up and down, in a flowing, sparkling red dress. Ivy stood beside her, in a more grown-up red dress and little white jacket. The preteen had her sister firmly by one hand, and the other hand clutching Fluff. Somehow they'd gotten the dog to wear a bow, and she was certain it had been Ivy's stubborn doing. Zoe would have to ask her about it later. She'd never once gotten her own terrier, Oz, to wear a bow without him promptly tearing it to pieces.

Then she saw Leo, standing tall in the pretend crow's nest of the pretend boat, and her breath caught in her throat. He was wearing a dress uniform, just like he had on the night they'd met. A pair of mirrored aviator sunglasses shielded his face from the sun, but she could tell he was scanning the crowd. He'd gotten a haircut since she'd seen him last. Not quite military buzz, but short in a way that accentuated the strength of his face and the lines of his jaw, yet still left just enough on top for a woman to run her fingers through. A flush rose to her cheeks at the thought. What was she doing letting herself think that way?

"Oh! Excuse me." A woman jostled her slightly, bumping into Zoe's table. "I'm so sorry."

The table wobbled. Zoe turned. The woman was in her twenties, in a hot-pink yoga outfit, tinted sunglasses and a mop of blond curls that cascaded all the way down her waist.

"No problem," Zoe said. "These tables are pretty unsteady. You're not the first."

The woman had a steaming cup of something that smelled like vanilla hazelnut coffee in her hand and a British tabloid tucked under her arm. She set both down in front of Zoe, then leaned her elbows on the table to steady it.

"Not a bad-looking man, is he? That navy guy." The blonde stranger smiled, and leaned in. "I was just reading that he's going to be the hot ticket item in a bachelor auction this weekend. Makes me wish I had a good amount of jingle in my pocket."

A bachelor auction? Really? Leo had just told them it would be an auction to raise money for building children's hospitals, but had said nothing about the bachelor part. Did Leo have any idea how incredibly difficult that was going to make their jobs as bodyguards? They'd have no way of knowing who was going to bid on him or who would win the special date, not to mention how to watch his back while he was with the woman in question. He'd been very clear with her that he'd promised Marisa he'd avoid any romantic entanglements until his daughters were grown.

"No, I didn't know that," Zoe said, feeling her smile tighten. "I don't read gossip."

She turned back to the window. Leo's float moved closer. Cheers rose around it, like a wave of noise accompanying it down the street. The earpiece had gone silent again and she wasn't about to open the link unless there was an actual emergency. The float finally rolled past. Leo's back was to her again. Zoe exhaled, as if she'd been holding her breath ever since she'd seen him coming. Why did this moody, complicated, distant man have such an effect on her? Was it because he was the best-looking man she'd ever laid eyes on? Was it because whenever he did let his guard down long enough to let her look inside all she could see was pain? He was like a lone warrior who'd spent his whole life struggling from battle to battle, and needed someone to watch his back so he wouldn't have to fight alone. Even though he'd made it clear she wasn't the kind of backup that he wanted.

She leaned back in her chair and stretched. Thankfully, the blonde had wandered off, but she'd left both her empty take-out cup and tabloid on the table. Zoe grabbed the cup, crumpled it into her hand and tossed it across the room into the garbage can. She made the shot without even hitting the rim. Then she glanced down at the tabloid and almost snorted at the headline glaring up at her.

Captain Darius Told: Forget that Woman from the Fire!

Pitiful. He was a commander, not a captain, first of all. The words were accompanied by a picture of her and Leo leaping from the castle fire. The image was so grainy that if it wasn't for her fluttering skirt there was no way to even guess she was female, let alone recognize her. The cover told her that story continued on page three. Her common sense told her that she should really toss it in the garbage without reading further. Her curiosity won. She turned to page three.

Is Canada's Favorite Naval Widower Out to Catch a New Mother for His Children?
Special by Killian Lynch

Something inside her balked. Anger burned in the pit of her stomach and she turned it into prayer. *Lord, it's so unjust. How do I cope with knowing Killian's star keeps rising when he's such an odious person? How do I let my anger go?*

When she'd been a teenager, she'd told herself that one day Killian Lynch would get his just deserts for how he treated people. She used to recite a Bible verse in her heart, every time he harassed and taunted her, about how God wasn't fooled. But now, years later, it felt like no matter what he did he was bulletproof. Sure, he was a creep who'd harassed women, wrote sensationalist headlines that distorted the truth and even now had a reputation for goading people into losing their temper just to grab damaging quotes and pictures of them. But he was still a minor celebrity. And she was a nobody.

She knew she should throw the magazine into the garbage. Instead, her eyes scanned the page. It wasn't so much a news article as a tribute to just how amazing Leo was and how so many beautiful, eligible women had posted comments online about how they'd like to be Leo's wife and the mother of his girls. Words spilled down the page outlining Leo's accomplishments, battles, medals and his heroic actions, and highlighting the impressive attributes of the beautiful, educated, wealthy and talented women who might show up at the bachelor auction to bid for him.

Lord, I know I shouldn't be reading this. I know I shouldn't let this infect me. But it does. And it hurts. Help me not to sabotage my peace and my confidence.

She prayed, even as she felt herself losing the battle to keep reading, just like she used to read the negative press about her years ago, back when critical words hurt like physical pain, causing her to skip meals, exercise too hard and push herself too far past her physical limits. She kept reading, like someone sabotaging her healthy habits by splurging on food they didn't even like the taste of, even as she felt herself teetering back into the darkness of low self-esteem and insecurity.

She reached the last line. It was continued onto another page. She bit her lip and flipped.

Black marker scrawled thick across the page, in a huge storm cloud and forks of lightning. *The Anemoi.*

Zoe leaped to her feet. Her eyes darted around the café. The blonde was nowhere to be seen. "Alex, Leo, we've got a problem. Someone dropped a magazine with a storm cloud drawn in it on my table."

"Do you have eyes?" Alex asked.

"No." Zoe pushed her way out onto the patio. Desperately she scanned the crowd. How had she been so distracted? How had she missed the threat?

"Another taunt or a specific warning?" Leo asked.

"A taunt. A picture of a storm cloud drawn on a tabloid article about you. Woman who dropped it on my table had hot-pink workout clothes, a pink baseball cap and lots of long, curly blond hair."

"Pandora again in a new disguise?" Alex asked.

"Probably." And she'd missed it. A flash of pink appeared through the crowd to her right. She hopped off the patio and pushed her way along the sidewalk. "Okay, I think I've got eyes. I'm going after her."

"Stay safe," Alex said. "Don't let it get to you."

She knew what he meant, but how could she not let it get to her? The woman had played her, taunted her and made a fool out of her. Not to mention clearly recognized her as someone Leo knew. People pressed thick around her. She pushed through the crowd, focusing on the blond curls and pink cap. She felt like an idiot. Alex had always said that nobody could beat Zoe up half as bad as she beat herself up. But this time, she deserved it.

"When do we alert police?" Alex asked.

"Like Leo said, it's just someone taunting us. It's criminal harassment, nothing more." She pressed forward. The towering fake naval ship floated down the road ahead of her. "I suggest we find a cop here and see if we can get them to help us detain her. How soon until you reach the fairgrounds?"

"Maybe twenty," Alex said. "But I don't have eyes on you."

"I'm following you up the street. I'm nearing the arch. There's an officer directing traffic at the next side street."

The woman started to jog. Zoe dashed after her, pushing through the crowd.

"I don't want you engaging when I can't see you," Alex said.

"It's okay," she said. "I've reached a cop."

He was tall and thin, with blond hair and a goatee.

"Excuse me, Officer, I need your help." Words spilled over each other in their rush to get out. "That woman in the pink hat just threatened Commander Leo Darius."

"It's nice to finally meet you, Zoe Dean." The cop's voice was a low hiss, cutting through the babble of the crowd. Then she felt the unmistakable tip of a gun pressing into her stomach. "I really don't want to hurt you, but I'm afraid I'm going to have to ask you to come with me. Just do what I tell you, come quietly and you won't get killed."

"Who are you?" Her hands rose slowly. "Where are you taking me?"

The crowd was still jostling around her, oblivious to the danger she was in. She could hear Alex and Leo now, shouting in her ear. But in an instant a rough hand yanked the earpiece out of her ear from behind and a second gun dug hard into the small of her back. She glanced over her shoulder.

"Prometheus," she said. She glanced back at the cop. "I'm guessing that makes you Jason of the Argonauts."

A gun to her front, a second gun to her back, and there she was trapped in the middle. People streamed past them on either side—families, small children, senior citizens. She'd taken out criminals with weapons before. But never two at once and not with innocent bystanders on every side.

As if reading her mind, Prometheus chuckled. "Now, you're coming with us. If you try anything, we'll fire into the crowd and people will die. Is that what you want?"

No. No, she didn't. She was being kidnapped in public, with no way to reach the rest of her team, and dozens of innocent people all around her as potential collateral.

Help me, Lord. What do I do? How do I escape?

She'd walked into a trap.

SEVEN

"Alex!" Leo's eyes scanned the crowd below him. "What's happening? Where is she?"

"I don't know," Alex said. "I know what you know. She's in danger. She was talking to a fake cop. She said something about being kidnapped, and I don't have eyes."

Leo could tell Zoe's brother was struggling to keep the panic he was feeling from his voice. He looked down. Alex was standing in the bow of the fake boat with Theresa, their bodies forming a protective shelter around Leo's girls as they smiled and waved at the crowd. The parade was slowing. The fairgrounds were only a few minutes ahead now.

Please, God! Help Zoe! Help me find her!

He'd lost eyes on her, too, now, and the irony of that killed him. He'd noticed her sitting on the coffee shop patio even before the float had made it halfway down the street. No matter how many times he'd told himself to look away after that something had kept drawing his eyes back to her, time and again, like a moth to a flame. She'd always been there, lurking just out of the corner of his eye. Now she was gone and everything in him needed to find her.

The float stopped again. The crowd moved. Then he saw her. She was walking along a thin alley between two buildings. Two men were with her.

"I saw her!" Leo said. "She's in a network of alleys behind the stores. I see two hostiles."

"Thank You, God," Alex whispered a prayer. Then he said, "Okay, I still can't see her, so I'm going to need you to direct me on how to find her. Do I leave the girls here with Theresa and go after Zoe right away? Or do I wait for you to climb down here to secure the girls and then try to find Zoe?"

Both were bad options. Theresa was an excellent therapist but she wasn't a bodyguard, and if Leo climbed down he'd lose his vantage point, not to mention they'd lose valuable time. He watched as Zoe and her kidnappers reached the end of the alley and turned into another one. The parade moved forward again. He lost her again.

"I've lost eyes." Leo groaned.

"Can you direct me?"

"Not well enough to risk Zoe's life on it," Leo said, "and I don't want you leaving the girls. We need a third option."

"Well I'm open to any ideas you've got. And I'm praying."

Leo was praying, too. The metal archway loomed ahead signaling that they were only fifteen minutes away from the end of the parade. That was fifteen minutes too long. He needed to go after her now. The commander's eyes rose to the heavens. "I can't believe I'm saying this, but I'm going to go after her."

"How?"

"I'm going to take the archway to the roof. Then I'll be able to search the alleys from above."

"That's a really bad idea," Alex said. He sounded slightly impressed.

The float rolled forward and he saw Zoe again. Her kidnappers pushed her down another narrow alley. A car blocked the end. Its trunk opened.

"I know. But I've got eyes again and the kidnappers have a car. Staying up high is the only way to maintain visual. It's rooftops or nothing. If I wait until the cherry picker reaches the ground I'll lose any hope of finding her."

The archway was just a few feet ahead of him now.

"You leaping from the top of the parade float is going to cause a pretty big scene. I'm just saying."

Yeah, he knew. But it was that or letting criminals take Zoe.

"I wouldn't do it if there was any other way." Leo braced his legs.

The archway grew closer. Ten feet. Eight feet.

"Just promise me you'll protect my daughters."

Six feet. Four feet.

"I will," Alex said. "With my life. You have my word."

"Don't let them worry. Tell them I'll be fine."

Two feet.

"I will," Alex said. "Please, save my sister."

"I will." Leo leaped.

He grabbed the bottom of the archway with both hands. His legs swung in thin air. The float disappeared beneath him. Voices shouted. He gritted his teeth, blocked them out, and pulled himself up to his feet. The ledge was so thin he could barely get more than his toes on and a fingertip grip. He worked his way sideways across the arch, feeling an old, familiar muscle ache. It had been a long, long time since he'd done basic training, and the regular physical fitness test he got now was nowhere near as exciting as the crazy obstacles he used to scale back then. But despite the danger and despite the risk, he felt strangely alive in a way he hadn't in a very long time.

He dropped down onto the rooftop and ran toward the alley. Later the full impact of what this meant for his cover and work with Admiral Jacobs would hit him. But for now the sound of the crowd faded to the back of his mind as his ears focused on one crystal clear sound ahead of him: Zoe was screaming.

He could see the end of the roof looming ahead of him. Just six feet, maybe seven lay between him and the next rooftop ahead of him. His footsteps sped up. He hit the edge of the rooftop and jumped, feeling the empty air surround him as he threw his body forward.

Zoe's screams echoed up from somewhere ahead of him: screams of fear, screams of determination and strength, the yells of a warrior fighting for her life.

I'm coming Zoe! Just hang on! He hit the roof and pitched forward into a front roll, barely managing to regain his balance before he reached the edge of the second roof. He crouched and looked down.

Prometheus had grabbed Zoe from behind. His arms clenched around her throat pulling her backward toward the car. Jason was standing by the trunk, at the ready to shut her inside.

"Leave her alone!" The three words flew from Leo's mouth with the strength and force of bullets firing inside him. He leaped over the edge of the roof and onto the fire escape. His feet pounded down the steps. Jason dove for the car. Prometheus yanked Zoe against him in a choke hold and opened fire. Bullets flew wild and unsteady, ricocheting off the fire escape and the metal garbage cans below. Below him he could see Zoe thrashing and struggling against Prometheus, even as he fired inches away from her head. They weren't going to take her. Leo wasn't going to let them. Not while he had a beat left in his chest. Leo vaulted over the end of the fire escape and let his body drop, landing hard on the dirty cement, and then rolled behind a Dumpster.

"Stop it!" Jason snapped. "You can't kill him! Darius has to stay alive!"

Leo didn't even let himself pause to think what that could mean. He threw his shoulder into the metal Dumpster and pushed. It rolled down the alley, bullets clanged futilely against the side.

"Dude!" Jason's voice rose to a shriek. "Come on! Let's go!"

Then Leo heard a click. Prometheus's gun was out of bullets. Leo wasn't about to let him reload. He dove around the Dumpster and charged. But before he could even get there, Zoe reached up and dug her nails into the huge thug's face. Prometheus swore, and threw Zoe to the ground. Leo caught him in the jaw and knocked him to the ground. Prometheus scrambled up and ran for the car.

"Zoe!" Leo crouched down beside her. Her clothes were torn. Blood streaked her arm from a nasty-looking scratch. "Look at me, baby, please. Are you okay?"

"Leo?" Her forehead crinkled like she wasn't sure it was really him. "What are you doing here?"

I'm rescuing you, silly. He opened his mouth to speak but no words came out.

The car lurched backward toward them.

It was heading straight for them. There was no time to run.

Leo threw his arms around Zoe.

They rolled. Zoe felt Leo's arms around her, sheltering her body. The car roared closer. The stench of exhaust smoke filled her lungs. Their bodies hit the alley wall. The car smacked against the Dumpster with a deafening ring that seemed to fill the alley and reverberate through her bones. The car lurched forward again. He saw Prometheus in the driver's seat and heard Jason yelling at him to stop.

For a heartbeat, Leo held her there, flat against the brick, shielding her, keeping his body between her and the car. Then she heard the screech of tires and the roar of the engine as the car pealed out of the alley. She looked up. They were gone.

"You okay?" He climbed to his feet. "Are you hurt? Do you need me to carry you?"

"I'm fine." Zoe grabbed his hand and pulled herself up. "I'm going after them."

But his grip tightened on her hand. "No, you're not."

"There are only a limited number of ways to get back to the highway. I mapped this area. I can chase them down and cut them off."

"And then you'll do what exactly? Drag them out of the car? Stop them all by yourself?"

"Yes!" She was breathing so fast that her whole body trembled. "Yes, I would. If that's what it takes to figure out who these people are and why they're after you. We have to stop them before they hurt you and your daughters."

Leo didn't answer. He just stood there and looked at her, like she was some wild, fierce, unbelievable creature he didn't know what to do with. His voice deepened. "You're injured."

"Trust me, I've dealt with far worse." She shivered and realized her voice was quaking. "I'm fine."

She didn't know why her body was shaking or why she was still clutching his hand as if he was the only thing keeping her from drowning.

"You're going to have a bruise in the morning." He reached up with his other hand. His fingers brushed the side of her face. "Look, if I can't convince you not to run into danger, then how about the argument that I just saved your life and I'd appreciate it if you didn't just throw it away again by chasing after some criminals intent on killing you."

"I'm pretty sure they wanted to take me alive."

"Is that supposed to make me feel better?" The fingers on his left hand traced the lines of her face. He pulled his right hand free of hers and slid it around her waist. He pulled her into his chest. "There's no way I was going to let them take you."

Zoe's hands crept up around his neck. "They shot at you."

"They were just trying to scare me off." His fingers ran along the edge of her jaw, tilting her face toward his. "I told you, I don't scare easily."

He brought her face closer. Her eyes closed, and she felt his lips brush slowly over her forehead then down over the bruise forming on her cheek. She shivered into him. Then he brought her lips up to meet his.

"Zoe! Leo! Are you alright?" Alex was pelting down the alleyway toward them, flanked by police.

They leaped apart. But still her eyes lingered on Leo's for a long minute, looking for some kind of sign of what had just happened. He'd been holding her. He'd been just about to kiss her. And she'd been about to let him. Did he have any idea how terrified she'd been? Or how much it had meant to her that he'd run to her rescue? But it was like the steel trap had closed over the depths of his eyes again, locking her out.

"I'm fine," Zoe called. She turned and ran toward her brother. There had to be at least six officers, both male and female, flanking him. "There were two men. Prometheus and Jason. They both had guns. They were driving a brown sedan without a readable license plate. They tried to kidnap me. Leo…" She took a breath and tried to visualize her heartbeat slowing. "Commander Darius came to my aid."

Aid was a safer word than *rescue*. She didn't want to think of him as rescuing her. It was too personal. Too close.

"My daughters?" Leo asked. He brushed past her, and something caught inside her heart at the depth and meaning that resonated in those two words. "Where are my daughters?"

"They're safe," Alex said. He raised both hands in reassurance. "Very, very safe. They're with Theresa, sitting right inside at the official emergency services booths at the fairgrounds surrounded by a whole bunch of real, verified police, paramedics and firefighters, who are finding them absolutely delightful and charming. They might as well have their own private army."

Leo nodded. "What about the fact I leaped from the parade float?"

Zoe blinked. He'd leaped from the parade float? She'd been so relieved to see him she hadn't even stopped to think about how he'd gotten there so quickly.

"Theresa told them you'd gone to get Zoe. They seemed to accept that as an answer. They seem to really like Zoe. Theresa also convinced the parade marshal to keep the parade going. People seem to think it was some kind of planned publicity stunt."

"Okay, thanks," he said. He turned his eyes to the sky and a long breath left his lungs. Then he looked at the police. "I'd like to see my daughters right away. So, while we need to file a report, I'd like to do it back at the fairgrounds once I've confirmed they're okay."

His voice was polite and calm, yet carried a firm, unmistakable authority that made it clear he expected the officers were going to agree. It was so easy to imagine the type of leader he'd been. He was the kind of man others would follow into danger without question. There was something undeniably attractive about it. They started walking back to the fairgrounds. Leo led the way with a few of the officers. She and Alex followed behind, walking through the side streets.

"I need you to tell me what happened," Alex said.

"There's not much to tell." She looked straight ahead. "I was following Pandora through the crowd. Prometheus and Jason ambushed me. They yanked out my earpiece, stuck two guns in my ribs, and told me if I didn't go with them they'd open fire on the crowd. I waited until we were away from innocent civilians and fought back."

She could still remember hearing the click of the trunk opening and the sight of the duct tape and zip ties lying inside. She shook her head, shaking away the terrifying moment and where it could have led.

"And then?" Alex prompted.

"And then Leo showed up," she said. "How did he get there so quickly?"

"He leaped onto the town arch and climbed across it."

They reached the end of the street. The brightly colored tents and canopies spread ahead of them, filling the park. Then she saw Eve and Ivy, seeming so small and fragile in comparison to the strength of the men and women in uniform around them. She watched as Leo's long strides turned into a jog as he hurried toward them, and heard the shouts of joy as the girls ran toward him. Leo dropped to one knee and swept Eve into a hug, while Ivy stopped just short, letting his hand brush her shoulder.

"Prometheus opened fire at Leo, but Jason told him they weren't supposed to kill him," she added. "Prometheus did try to hit us with the car, though. But again, I got the impression from Jason they need him alive."

She wasn't looking at her brother. She was looking at Leo. He glanced back, over his shoulder, and for one second Zoe felt his gaze brush her face. A shiver ran down her spine. Leo turned away and the small family walked back to the emergency services booth.

"I've rescued a lot of people in my life," Alex said, "but I don't normally clutch them like that afterward. I can't have your back if I don't know what's going on with you."

What did he expect her to say? That she was attracted to Leo? That she couldn't get him out of her mind? That for the first time in her life it felt like her heart had woken up and started wishing for a dozen different things her mind knew it could never have?

"Talk to me." There was the hint of something firm in Alex's voice. "Please. I know what I saw."

"Leo told me that he promised his late wife that he'd never bring another woman into his daughters' lives until they were grown," she said. "He made that very clear. But according to the article that The Anemoi scribbled on, this event you're accompanying Leo to tomorrow is a bachelor auction, and there's a big long list of eligible women who are eager to be the next Mrs. Darius."

Alex sucked in a breath. "I had no idea."

"Neither did I." She turned and looked up at her big brother. "So, whatever you're thinking right now, don't say it. If you want to protect me, you'll forget what you saw. Leo is our client, a national hero, a widower and the single father of two remarkable children. He's completely closed off, like he's afraid of ever trusting again, and has made it clear he doesn't want me getting too close. So I'm going to keep my distance, focus on doing my job and help make sure those girls and their dad are safe. And that's it."

No matter how deeply the memory of his lips almost touching hers might be seared on her brain.

EIGHT

For a moment she thought Alex was going to argue with her. But then she saw the beautiful, willowy form of Alex's fiancée, Theresa, walking across the grass toward them. Theresa waved. Zoe smiled and waved back.

"Also, I'm not in the mood for a therapy pep talk from Theresa right now, either," she added quickly. "I'll deal with this my way."

"Got it," Alex said. "Don't worry. I've got your back. And if you need anything, I'm here."

"I know. Thanks." Zoe slipped away through the fairgrounds, her eyes roaming unseeingly over the stands and booths. She knew she'd have to return to the emergency services booth soon to file a report about what had happened. Then she and Alex would have to sit down and strategize their plan for the charity auction, not to mention disrupting Josh's honeymoon yet again to fill him in on the kidnapping attempt. But she'd give herself five minutes first. Five minutes to walk, calm her heart, settle her nerves and pray. Five minutes to erase the memory of Leo's hands on her waist and his lips on her face.

"Zoe! Zoe Dean! Is that really you?" An Irish voice

shouted behind her. She spun around, hands raised, as her body reacted to the voice before her mind even had a moment to process who was calling her name. Killian Lynch, blogger and life-wrecker was running toward her, a cell phone raised high in his hand like a grenade whose pin he was just waiting to pull. She froze, hands still in front of her, feeling the urge to run pouring over her like panic. Why did this one obnoxious man affect her this way? She hadn't spoken to him since the day that had effectively ended her competitive career, although she'd gotten plenty of press coverage afterward, of him laughing off the notion that a weak, little girl like her had actually hurt him. There'd almost been something twisted in the way he made a point of the fact he'd barely felt the blow and yet seemed to maintain a personal vendetta that pushed the idea she should be dropped from competing. Even now, there was something about just being near him that set her teeth on edge.

"Don't hit me!" He laughed loudly and waved his hands in mock surrender. "I remember how slap happy you are. But I promise I come in peace!"

He stopped just a couple of feet in front of her. She lowered her hands. But she didn't meet his eye. He was wearing a tweed jacket and tie with a pair of jeans that somehow looked both very casual and very expensive.

"Wow, isn't this a blast from the past?" he asked. "I can't believe I didn't recognize you the night of the castle fire."

But he had recognized her now, from a distance, across a crowded field? Killian sounded more irritated than amazed. She didn't even know how to answer. The whole thing was suspicious. Had someone else tipped him off to who she was? Or had he figured it out on his own?

Either way, it seemed he was playing off the blow to his face that she once thought had ruined her like it was some kind of hilarious joke.

"Yep, it's me." Even with her hands down at her sides, she could feel her fingers involuntarily close into fists. "What do you want?"

"I just wanted to give you the opportunity to comment on tonight's blog before it went viral."

"Whatever it's about, the answer is 'No comment.'"

"So you're denying that you're in a secret, romantic relationship with Commander Leo Darius, and his entry in the charity bachelor auction is nothing but a sham?" he asked.

"What?" Despite herself she could feel the hackles rising on the back of her neck. "Are you kidding me?"

"Does he know about your past?" Killian asked. He leaned in, sticking the cell phone microphone in her face. "Did you put him up to that crazy stunt of leaping onto the arch like that? How does he feel about having someone potentially unstable in his daughters' lives?"

"I'm not about to comment on something so totally ridiculous." Zoe turned and walked away, her hand swatting the air around her in frustration like she was trying to escape a spider's web. If he wanted to publish garbage she couldn't stop him, but she wasn't about to help him.

"Do the girls know you're dating?" Killian followed after her. "How do they feel about having a new woman in their daddy's life?"

"You're disgusting." Zoe didn't turn.

"I have pictures!" Killian called. "Got them not five minutes ago."

"You what?" Zoe's footsteps froze. An odd sense of fear filled her limbs. "I don't know what kind of sick joke you think you're playing—"

"It's not a joke!" Killian cut her off. He stretched out his hand and tilted the phone toward her. "These go live at midnight."

She stared down at the screen. There were two pictures, extreme close-ups, of her and Leo together. In the first, his hand was on her cheek. In the second, he was leaning in like he was about to kiss her. His face was partly blocked by the angle and the shadows, and the photos were so tightly cropped it was impossible to tell where they were. But there was no mistaking the look on her face or the light shining in her eyes. She looked like a woman who was infatuated. She looked like a woman who just might even be at risk of falling in love. "Where did you get these?"

"Do you deny these are you?" Killian asked.

No, she didn't deny it. It was her and Leo, alone in the alley, just moments ago, after Jason and Prometheus had fled. Judging by the angle and the quality they had to have been taken by an aerial drone.

"I'll ask you again, where did you get these pictures?" Her eyes locked on the phone, wondering what would happen if she pulled it from his hand. "Was it you? Was it another journalist? Did you get any pictures of what happened before this or of the other people in the alley or the car?"

Did he have pictures of the attack? Did he have pictures that the authorities could use to identify members of The Anemoi?

"I don't have to tell you that," he said. "I just showed you these as a courtesy."

He was grinning at her, like he'd managed to outsmart her, and she wished she could wipe the smugness off his face.

"Answer the question." Zoe lowered her voice and stepped closer. "Because I promise you the police are going to want to know."

"You can go ahead and report me to the police, but they won't touch me. It's freedom of the press and I'm a guest in this country."

"Not if you've been using a drone to secretly follow and photograph a national hero! And not if you have evidence of a crime."

His jaw clenched. Then he yanked the cell phone back and tapped the screen. It buzzed.

"Whatever. I just posted them online. They're live now. Why wait for the story? After all, a picture's worth a thousand words."

Zoe felt her face fall. Killian smirked.

"Go run to the police," he added. "Tell them I won't take them down without a legal injunction, and by then they'll be all over the internet anyway and I'll have left the country. And as far as crime is concerned, whatever you mean by that, I only had two pictures and they came from an anonymous source."

The dread in Zoe's stomach grew tighter. "What source?"

"An anonymous source," he repeated. His grin grew teeth. "So if I were you, I'd go tell your boyfriend that someone is spying on him and it isn't me."

A warm night breeze slipped through the bedroom window, brushing the bottom of the pink floral curtains. As Leo leaned over Eve's bed to hug his daughter good-night, he felt her latch around his neck and squeeze so tightly he was surprised her young arms had that much strength.

"Don't go away, Daddy," she said. "Stay with us. Please."

He swallowed hard and accepted the hug. It had been a long drive back to their home in Ottawa. The chaos at the parade meant that Leo hadn't been approached by his contact, leaving the auction his last opportunity to meet the informant and receive the intel. He'd also talked to Josh, who in the light of the news had decided to abandon his honeymoon two days early and make up the time later. Josh and Samantha would now take the girls to Cedar Lake tomorrow.

"I'm not going anywhere," he said. "You and your sister are going to a cottage for one night without me— just one—while I go to my work event. You'll get there with Josh and Samantha at nighttime, get tucked into bed, and then when you wake up in the morning I'll be there. Then we'll have a whole week together, just swimming and hiking, and having fun."

"I wish you were coming with us," Eve said in a quiet voice. She let go of his neck.

"I do, too," Leo admitted. He sat back, on the edge of her bed, and looked down at her wrapped in blankets and surrounded by a herd of pastel stuffed animals. "But I'll be there before you wake up in the morning. I promise."

Ivy snorted loudly behind him. When did she learn to do that? Was that something all preteens suddenly woke up knowing how to do the moment they turned twelve? "Don't bother trying to argue with him, Eve, or asking him to stay. It won't work."

He turned. Ivy was curled up on a mattress on the floor in the corner of Eve's room. When he'd bought the beautiful family home in downtown Ottawa last year he'd hoped Ivy would be thrilled to finally have her own room. She'd spent days choosing paint and picking out furniture. Yet, in the middle of that first night, she'd dragged her bedding and mattress into her little sister's much smaller room and set up camp near the end of her bed. He didn't know why. But there'd been such a defiance in her eyes when he'd tried to ask about it that he'd decided to back off and let her tell him when she was ready. Now, keeping with tradition, Fluff had ignored his fancy dog bed on the landing and instead slept curled up on the mattress beside Ivy. "What makes you say that?"

Ivy was looking at her sister, and not at him. "Trust me, Eve, asking Daddy not to go away never works. He says he'll stay, but he won't."

Ivy's voice was serious, like she was trying to break bad news to her sister gently. Eve's eyes went wide and filled with tears. Leo was torn between following his instinct to tell Ivy to shut it, and listening to hear what she was going to say. Zoe's words from the parking lot echoed in his heart. Ivy had a reason for leaping in the river after Fluff without telling him. She had a reason for saying something so bizarre and worrying to Eve now. But he didn't know what it was or how to get her to trust him.

Lord, what happened to close her heart this way? Help me know what to do.

"I promise you, it's only for one night," he said

firmly, looking from Ivy to Eve. "I promise. One hundred percent. And you'll have fun. You can take Fluff. Josh and Samantha are going with you—"

"Is Zoe coming up with you?" Ivy asked. "Or is she coming with us?"

"Yeah, can Zoe come to the cottage, too? Please?" Eve's voice chimed in.

"No," he said. "Neither. Zoe's not coming to the cottage."

Ivy sighed loudly, flopped back on the pillows and looked up at the ceiling. "Figures."

What kind of response was that? What did it even mean? "What figures?"

"Why can't Zoe come?" Eve asked again. "I saw her at the parade! I waved at her, but she didn't see me. I told you I wanted to talk to her."

In fact, Eve had practically tried to drag him across the grass to see her. But he'd hurried them out of the parade, to the car and home again, as soon as he'd spoken to police.

Ivy rolled over onto one elbow. "Eve, I'm sorry, but I think Daddy doesn't want us to see Zoe anymore."

Eve gasped. What was this? What was going on here?

"What do you mean?" he asked Ivy, his voice sharper than he meant it to be. "Why did you say that?"

Ivy sighed loudly and fell backward into the pillow. "Never mind."

Don't push her, said a quiet voice in the back of his mind that sounded suspiciously like Zoe. *She'll tell you when she's ready.* But would she? Or would father and daughter just retreat to their quiet, stony corners, ignoring the weight of the unsaid words piled up be-

tween them? Suddenly, the thought of Zoe arguing toe
to toe with him in the pizza parlor parking lot flashed
in his mind, her eyes filled with fire and determination. He couldn't imagine Zoe ever agreeing to a quiet,
sad failure of a marriage like Marisa had. Zoe was a
fighter, one who he imagined had never given up on
anything that mattered to her without fighting for it
with all she had.

His phone buzzed. He looked down. The picture
of smiling, wholesome blonde Melody Young flashed
on his screen. As much as he hated Zoe's suggestion
that what had happened could have anything to do
with Marisa, he'd still sent her a message earlier in
the hopes that she'd be able to help fill in some of the
gaps about Marisa's life without him.

"Is that Zoe?" Eve asked.

"No." He slid his phone into his pocket. "It's a
friend of your mommy's called Melody Young. She
has twin boys. I was thinking I might invite them for
a visit while we're at the cottage."

Ivy went white. "We don't like her."

It seemed Ivy didn't like a lot of things these days.

"I don't remember her," Eve said.

"She took you for ice cream," Ivy said. "Remember?"

"No." Eve shook her head.

"Well, I haven't invited her yet and I won't invite
anyone without telling you." He could see Ivy's mouth
about to open again. He didn't have time for another
argument. "But right now, it's late and you need to
sleep. It's been a very long day."

He gave Eve a second hug, told both girls he loved
them, then slipped out into the hallway and closed the
door behind him, being careful to leave it open a crack

so the light still got in. He heard them whispering quietly as he walked down the stairs to the main floor. Thankfully, whatever they were whispering about was making Eve giggle.

His heart ached.

Lord, I love them so much. But I miss Marisa. She knew how to talk to them. She knew how to mother them. Help me be the parent they need me to be.

Hot summer air was seeping in through the crack in the living room window, smelling like the promise of rain. He'd have to go upstairs and close the girls' windows when he went to bed, so they wouldn't be scared or get wet when the thunderstorm hit. But for now, it could wait.

He slipped the front door open and stepped out into the night. The huge, wooden porch of his Ottawa home was one of his favorite things about living in Canada's capital city. He crossed the porch barefoot, in an old battered pair of jeans and a loose white T-shirt. His phone started ringing again. It was Melody. He answered. "Hello?"

"Commander Darius?" Her voice was cheerful, friendly and a bit breathless, as if talking to him rattled her nerves. "It's Melody Young."

"Hi, Melody." He smiled. "You can call me Leo."

"Oh. Okay. Thank you, Leo."

He dropped into a chair and took another look at the picture of Melody and Eve on his phone. Eve was probably about two in the picture, he guessed, maybe younger. Melody's hair was blond, too, a slightly lighter shade than Eve's and Marisa's natural gold. There was something very girl-next-door about Melody, from the blue jean skirt and flowered top she wore in the picture to the wide, cheerful smile. Everything about her reminded him of Marisa.

She was nothing like Zoe.

"Thank you for calling me back," he said.

"Oh, no problem! I just missed the girls so much. They're really beautiful. I was so sorry to hear about Marisa's passing."

"Thank you," he said. "How did you know Marisa?"

"We were next-door neighbors," she said. "I used to see the girls after school or bring over meals sometimes when I knew Marisa was working late. Sometimes she had me babysit. I was like a part of the family."

"And you have sons?" he asked.

"Two," she said. "Twins. They loved your girls. Especially Eve."

The sky was a deep blue above his head. The wide tree-lined street was silent. He closed his eyes and could hear the faint rumble of traffic in the distance, mingling with the roar of the Ottawa River not far away. How was he going to ask this woman if Marisa had enemies or addictions? Let alone if she'd had any relationships she hadn't told him about? It felt like a betrayal to her memory even to ask. Zoe's questions still burned in his mind, and he was no closer to having answers. Melody was cheerfully babbling on about her boys and his girls, the topic of conversation so very far away from the ugly questions he had to ask.

"We're actually moving to Ottawa this September," Melody went on, "so the boys can be closer to their father. I can't remember if I told you, but I work in child care. I don't know what your situation's like, but if you need any extra help, I'd be happy to pick your girls up from school, sort them dinner and be with them at your house until you get home from work. If that's the kind of thing you're looking for. Right now I work for a single mother in Winnipeg, and I'm sure she'd be happy to provide references."

She had no idea how tempting an idea that was. A caregiver for his girls would make it so much easier to shield them from the more dangerous parts of his work. If Ivy was able to get over her jealousy, or whatever it was that had added Melody onto her list of people she wasn't impressed with. There was something appealing about knowing the girls had another motherly figure in their lives who'd pick them up from school, care for them, make meals and share the burden.

Melody launched into a story about baking with his daughters, but he was only half listening, as an intense and sudden sorrow for the loss of Marisa swept over him like a wave. He missed Marisa. Yes, she hadn't been in love with him. Yes, their relationship had missed the kind of romance that marriages were supposed to be founded on. But she'd been stable. She'd been caring. She'd been real. At least that's how she'd always seemed to be. Would it be so wrong to create that kind of life again? To find someone who he wasn't romantically involved with, and would never pursue a relationship with, who'd nevertheless be a caregiver for his girls?

Can Zoe come with us?

Eve's innocent question suddenly floated in the back of his mind. A long sigh left his body that seemed to come from the depths of some cavern deep inside. Zoe was the opposite of either a Marisa or a Melody.

Zoe tackled life with a fight, intensity and passion that was both exhilarating and exhausting to watch. It was like Zoe's energy had infected him, making him leap off a parade float and sprint toward armed criminals to save her. He'd risked his mission over her. He'd come so close to kissing her. He'd been tempted to break his promise to Marisa. He'd put himself in danger. He'd put his heart in danger.

What's more, something deep inside him had enjoyed every moment of it—like he'd been thirsty for years and Zoe was offering him his first drink of water.

"Leo?" Zoe's voice floated to him, on the hot summer's night's air, cutting through Melody's voice in his ear. He jerked upright and opened his eyes. There Zoe stood, on his sidewalk in front of his house, in a flowing white sundress that stopped just below the knees. She walked toward him, slowly, like something out of a dream. He stood. Her dark hair was wild and loose around her heart-shaped face. Wind brushed the trees around her, sending the dark leaves clattering and tossing her skirt around her strong slender legs.

She was beautiful. And captivating. And inaccessible. And perfect.

He knew in that moment, without the shadow of a doubt, that he'd never seen anything more gorgeous in his entire life than Zoe walking slowly up the grass lawn toward him in the fading summer light.

"I'm so sorry, Melody," he said. "I've got to go. I'm going to be at a friend's cottage for a few days. But I'm hoping we can get together to talk more about Marisa soon and maybe even have you and your sons come up to visit us at the cottage. I'm really glad we connected."

Melody said that she understood and they exchanged goodbyes, but his mind barely registered it as he hung up the phone and slid it into his pocket. His eyes stayed locked on Zoe, and hers on him as if, if either of them blinked, the other would suddenly be gone. Zoe reached the porch. He stood. "When did you guys get back?"

"Not too long ago," she said. She walked up the steps toward him. Golden light of his front porch light drenched her limbs. "I'm sorry to drop by so late and unannounced, but Alex and I needed to talk to you urgently. He's just parking the Ash Security van now. We have reason to think you're under surveillance."

"Surveillance?" The word washed over him like a bucket of cold water. He'd worked so hard, jumped through every hoop and taken every precaution to make sure his work remained a secret. The idea that someone had been watching, following him, even photographing, destroyed all that in an instant. If he didn't find out who had him under surveillance and why, his work with internal intelligence would be over.

She looked up at the thick canopy of trees shielding them from view.

"We don't know how far spread it is," she said. "Or what was involved. But we have to assume that whoever's been watching you knows about the informant and that you're after the intel."

Just moments ago, as he'd watched Zoe walk up the drive, he'd almost felt like he was in a dream. Now it seemed his worst nightmare might be coming true.

NINE

"How did you find out?" Leo asked.

"Killian Lynch." Zoe stepped back against the privacy of the overhang. "He published pictures of us on his media website tonight." There was something off about her voice. Something odd. Almost strained. She held out her phone "They were taken today. He said they were emailed to him from an anonymous source. He's no doubt going to be adding some sensationalist story to go with them later."

He took the phone from her hand. His eyes scanned the screen. Heat rose to his neck. They were just hugging. Their lips hadn't even touched and yet...yet he looked like a man holding a woman he wanted to sweep into his arms and surrender his heart to.

"So, have you filled him in on the new plan?" Alex's voice wafted over the lawn.

Leo looked up. Zoe's brother was walking up his front walk.

"What plan?" he asked.

"Alex and Josh think that we should take advantage of the distraction this offers us," Zoe said. "They think I should go with you to the bachelor auction, as your date, and make sure I win the bid on you."

"Bachelor auction? What bachelor auction?" He laughed reflexively, even though it wasn't funny. He didn't know which part of that sentence was more ridiculous—the idea that he'd let random women bid on a date with him, or that Ash Private Security's solution was to take the one woman he was battling a romantic attraction to with every breath in his body, and toss her directly into his arms. "That's the most ridiculous thing I've ever heard. I still haven't received that package I was supposed to receive this week. I still have no idea who my contact is or what they look like. Tomorrow's auction is my last opportunity to get that intel. Now you're telling me tomorrow's event is actually a bachelor auction, I'm under surveillance, there are pictures of me and Zoe online, and your suggestion for how to handle all that is for Zoe to come to the auction and compete for me, like some kind of arm candy?"

"You think flitting around a boring, snobby event, bidding for you against other women is my idea of a good time?" Zoe said. The chill in her voice cut the laughter from his tongue. "Trust me, I have no desire to be arm candy or to fight other women for you. And while I might not be a spy, I do value my privacy and don't like being watched or having my photos online, either. But you said this is your last opportunity to meet your contact and get the intel you need. We promised to have your back and I will do my job, whether I feel like it or not."

He stepped back. Well, there was a blow to the ego if he'd ever had one. When she'd practically crumpled into his arms in the alleyway, he'd presumed that she was every bit as attracted to him as he was to her.

He didn't answer. She didn't say anything more. Alex didn't speak, either, and for a moment the air around them seemed to crackle with tension. Then he ran his hand over his face and tried to wipe the memory of her in his arms as far out of his mind as he could. His phone buzzed. He looked down. It was Killian.

"Why don't you both head into the living room, then we can sit down and talk this out? I have something to sort quickly." He waited until they'd gone inside, then looked at his phone.

Hey! Sorry about the online picture blast but I've been trying to meet up with you to go over this stuff I've got and you weren't around.

So the Irishman had given up on playing nice and was now trying to get his attention by posting surveillance photos of him and writing scandalous things about his personal life?

He texted back: I'm here now and I'm listening. What do you want?

A pause, then Killian wrote: I want to make a deal.

He responded: What kind of deal?

A deal for the intel because Killian was really his informant? Or an agreement to let him know who he'd gotten the surveillance pictures from because Killian was nothing more than a dupe being used by The Anemoi to rattle Leo's cage?

An expensive one. Hahaha! Killian's response told him nothing.

See you tomorrow, Leo replied, then put his phone back in his pocket.

He joined Alex and Zoe in the living room. The

desire to talk about the texts he'd gotten from Killian itched like an insect bite under his skin. But his admiral had promised the informant total anonymity. He couldn't risk blowing his informant's cover.

Even if it turned out to be Killian.

They sat and Alex briefed him on what the media was saying about the event and why they thought the best course of action was to take advantage of the media buzz around him and Zoe.

Leo still needed a second pair of eyes with him at the event, and also apparently now an excuse to get out of the bachelor auction Nigel had signed him up for. Having an attractive woman on his arm, who the media had already linked him to, who was also incredibly talented at both surveillance and combat fighting was a no-brainer. Leo would make it very clear to Nigel that he wasn't about to be auctioned off as a bachelor, but that he would still attend the event. Zoe would pose as his date. When it looked like anyone wanted to speak to Leo alone, he could count on Zoe to make herself scarce, to protect the informant's identity. The plan made a lot of sense. In fact the only thing stopping him from fully embracing the plan was his attraction to her.

"She'd be hidden in plain sight," Alex concluded. "No one is going to suspect she's anything but your date. We're taking this curveball Killian Lynch tossed at us and using it for our advantage. You'll have backup, cover and a second pair of eyes. Everything you needed and hired us for."

A warm breeze ruffled the curtains. Zoe was sitting opposite him on an ottoman, her elbows on her knees and her eyes looking everywhere but his face.

"I think it sounds like a really smart idea," Leo said, after a long moment. "Tactically speaking. But, first off, just to be clear, I really had no idea that tomorrow's event was a bachelor auction. None at all. All I told Nigel is that I was putting up a nice meal and tickets to a show. I never agreed to be anyone's...date." He floundered for words, then shrugged. "If I'd known that's what he had in mind, I never would've agreed to it. So, I'm sorry I laughed when you told me, Zoe. I was just shocked."

"No problem." Zoe looked up. She wasn't smiling, but she wasn't frowning anymore, either.

"Second," he went on, "now that I know it's being pegged as a bachelor auction I definitely won't be taking part. I agree that it would be a security nightmare. Not to mention it will be much harder for my contact to approach me if I'm caught up in a circus like that. I'll call Nigel tonight, and tell him to pull my name from the auction. So, don't worry. You won't have to bid on me."

He smiled, very slightly. So did she.

"Good. I only have two thousand, four hundred and twenty-eight dollars in the bank anyway, and I was saving up for a new car."

His eyebrow rose. "And you think a date will go for that much?"

"Probably not." Her smile grew larger and he could tell she was teasing him. "But I wouldn't want to risk it."

The room fell silent again. But the crackle in the air from before still seemed to linger.

"Right." Alex stood up. He looked from Leo, to

Zoe, and back again. "I need to make a phone call. I'll give you two a minute."

He excused himself and headed through a door to the kitchen, leaving Leo and Zoe alone. The door clicked behind him. Thunder rumbled far in the distance. The smell of impending rain deepened in the air.

"What's your take on this new plan?" Leo asked.

"I think you're right," she said. She frowned, "It's a smart plan."

"But you don't like it."

"I didn't say that."

She didn't have to.

"Be straight with me," Leo said. "Are you up to it?"

"Am I up to it?" Her eyes flashed with that familiar fire he was almost beginning to get attached to. "Are you seriously sitting there asking me if I'm up to doing my job?"

"No." He stood. "I'm asking you if you're okay going to a very fancy party, posing as my date tomorrow night? Because you don't look happy about it. Not at all. You don't survive commanding a boat full of people very long if you can't figure out when someone's feeling mutinous." She cut her eyes at him. Her frown deepened. "I'm sorry, that was the wrong word. What you look is frustrated."

"You think I'm frustrated?" she practically spluttered.

He could tell that she meant it rhetorically. But he decided to answer her anyway because he could see a deeper question lingering there in her eyes.

"Honestly?" He fixed his eyes on her, almost daring her to look away. "I think you're frustrated at the idea of being arm candy. In fact, something about that really bothers you."

She leaped to her feet. "Do you have any idea how insulting it is?"

"To be called arm candy?" His arms crossed. "No, of course not. I don't have a clue what it's like for you to be treated like some pretty little sweet thing, instead of seen for your intellect, courage or combat skills." He pointed his finger toward the top of the stairs, in the direction of where his girls now were somewhere between giggling and sleeping. "But I do know I'm the father of two incredible daughters, and it really matters to me that I don't raise them like that. I want to raise them to be strong, and confident, and smart, and to feel like they can take on the world. I want to raise them to be like you and I don't know how. Right now, I don't even feel like I'm succeeding at being a half-good parent. Ivy still isn't talking to me. She seems more upset at me than ever and it's hurting Eve, too. I wish they hadn't lost their mother. Because, despite all the problems we had in our failed, sad, hollow shell of a marriage, Marisa was a great mother who understood them, listened to them and could've helped them learn how to handle this world."

He dropped his arm again and looked down at Zoe. She was standing in front of him, in his own living room, her breath rising and falling quickly in her chest. And it suddenly hit him that he'd finally admitted to another human being what his marriage to Marisa had really been like. She hadn't been happy. Neither had he. Their marriage had been a hollow shell of what a relationship should be.

"I do miss Marisa," he added. His voice dropped.

He hadn't meant to blurt all that out to anyone, ever, let alone in a moment of frustration, and yet it also felt like he'd just let go of something heavy he was tired of carrying. "It wasn't a romance. Our marriage was a failure. We were separated when she died. But she was a really caring mother. She would've done anything for Ivy and Eve. And I wish the girls hadn't lost her."

He swallowed hard. Zoe's eyes teemed with unspoken words. But she didn't say anything. She just stood there, listening.

"I can't begin to pretend to know what it was like for you growing up in the media spotlight," he added. "And I still haven't read up about you online, because I want to get to know you, not what other people wrote about you. I promise you that no matter what the tabloids print or what people might think when we step out together, I for one will always know who you are and why you're really there with me. I promise you that. All right?"

"All right." She met his gaze and held it. The air seemed to crackle between them like electricity. Thunder roared louder.

"I've really got to go close the girls' bedroom window." Leo stepped back. Alex was standing behind them in the doorway, like he wasn't sure whether to come in or go out. "And I'm guessing you two need to get going."

They said their goodbyes and he showed them both out. Then he stood there, for a long moment, his hand still on the door handle. Had he made the right decision? Was it a mistake to agree to go to the auction tomorrow with Zoe on his arm?

He had to be strong and build reinforcements

around his heart. He had to remind himself that no matter what he thought and felt when Zoe was there beside him she would never be his. He'd let his guard down around her twice. The first time he'd pulled her into his arms and almost kissed her. The second he'd admitted the truth about his failed marriage with Marisa.

He couldn't let it happen again.

Zoe chose a purple dress for the party. It was a deep, rich color somewhere between indigo and the summer night sky. She ran her fingers through her hair, twisted strands around her face, tweaking them this way and that. She frowned. Was the dress too simple? It was a cocktail dress and she imagined most women would be in gowns. But gowns were impossible to run in and hard to modify for undercover work. Not to mention she'd pretty much destroyed her only good long dress for covert operations in the castle fire.

She carefully hid the bruise on her cheek with foundation. Then she added a touch of gray and gold to her eyes, then another light shimmer of color to her cheekbones, highlighting her natural tan. Was it enough makeup? Too much? Her mind still recoiled at the gobs of paint and glitter she'd been expected to wear on her face while doing gymnastics, and remembered the relief she'd found in doing martial arts where nobody cared how pretty someone was as long as they got the upper hand on the person attacking them. But now, she cared and didn't like thinking about why.

This wasn't a date. They'd both made that clear. No matter what kind of moment she'd thought they'd shared in the alley when he'd rescued her. Or what had flipped in her chest when their eyes had first met. Or what she'd felt roaring inside her last night, in his living room, when he'd told her that he'd understood her.

No matter what her own heart kept whispering to her.

Lord, why would You let me long for something I can never have? I've never felt this way about anyone. Why is the first man I've been attracted to this way someone I can't ever be with?

"Ready for your big night?" Alex called from the small living room of their two-bedroom hotel suite.

"Just about." On a whim, she spun around, watching the shimmering fabric rise and fall around her like a fountain. Eve would probably have loved it. She joined her brother in the living room. They took the elevator down to the ground floor and walked to the van. She hopped into the passenger seat. "Just to be clear, the only reason I'm not fighting you for who gets to drive is because I hate driving in heels."

"I know." Alex got in the driver's side. He started the van.

"And tonight is not a date," she said.

Alex's eyebrows rose. "I never said it was."

He didn't need to. They'd been best friends since they were kids. Probably even before the ink had dried on their parents' marriage certificate. But since they'd left Leo's house last night, there'd been this weird, awkward silence, accentuated by the feeling that when they were talking Alex was choosing his words so carefully it was like he was afraid she was a hand grenade ready to blow. The nondescript black van drove smoothly through the Ottawa streets. The beautiful château hotel where the auction was being held glittered ahead of them, copper and gold against the night sky. She punched her brother in the shoulder like she did when they were kids. "Talk to me. Something is clearly bothering you."

Alex stared straight ahead through the window. "You made it clear you don't want to talk about the Leo situation."

"Because there is no Leo situation—"

"Will you stop telling yourself that? Twice now I've walked in on you two staring each other down like you were each fighting some private battle in the other's eyes. But you're both too stubborn to admit it."

"I've told you it doesn't matter," Zoe said. "As my brother, you've always had my back, respected me and never once pushed me to talk about something I didn't want to talk about."

"Well, if you don't want me to get involved as your big brother, then let me talk to you as a colleague," Alex said. "You and I helped found Ash Private Security. We're the ones who convinced Josh to join the team. We made Ash Private Security what it is, and Commander Leo Darius is the biggest, most prominent client we've ever had. Daniel initiated a conference call between Josh and I this morning to ask if we thought you should be pulled off this assignment. He put it to a vote."

Her colleagues met behind her back to vote whether she should be pulled off an assignment? Anxiety climbed up inside her throat and when she spoke she felt her words coming out so sharply they could cut glass. "And?"

The light turned red in front of her. Alex braked. Then to her surprise he chuckled under his breath. "Do you think for a moment any one of us voted against you, sis? We know you. None of us could ever vote against you, Zoe. It was unanimous. We all back you. One hundred percent."

"Oh." She sat back against the seat, feeling slightly foolish and relieved by the reminder that her team was behind her. The light changed. Alex kept driving.

"But that doesn't mean we don't think your judgment is compromised."

"Nothing is ever going to happen between me and Leo," Zoe interjected.

"And you think that makes you less emotionally compromised, Zoe? You think pretending your heart doesn't exist keeps yourself from caring about someone? Because believe me, it doesn't. I've been through that with Theresa. Josh went through that with Samantha. It never works. It just tears you apart silently from the inside out."

Sudden tears brushed the edges of her eyes. *Lord, I don't know why I can't admit he's right. But thank You that he understands.*

The Ottawa hotel loomed above them. A surge of press crowded behind a red velvet rope. Limousines and luxury cars pulled up slowly, dropping off glamorous guests. They drove past them, into an alley and down a nondescript service delivery ramp to the parking garage where they'd go over the plan and meet up with Leo.

"So," Alex said. "After tonight is done, you and I are going to sit down and talk this through, just like we used to in the old days when something was bothering us. Or, if you'd rather, schedule a long talk with Theresa, pronto. She's not just your future sister-in-law, she's a really good psychotherapist and she loves you." He slowed as the ramp grew steeper beneath them. A rolling metal door rose ahead of them. He eased the van through, down another ramp and into a deserted cargo bay next to the service elevator. Then he cut the engine, and looked at her. "Talk to someone. It doesn't have to be me. But whatever it is going on inside you, you need to stop treating it like some secret battle you've got to fight all alone. We're all here for you. No matter what."

Sudden tears of gratitude rushed to her eyes. She didn't let them fall. How could she admit to them that it felt like she had some hopeless crush on some man who she couldn't have a future with? That she didn't feel good enough for him? That she didn't feel good enough to be the mother his amazing daughters so desperately needed?

"Okay." She smiled weakly. "Tonight, after this whole shindig, after Leo leaves to go up to Cedar Lake, you and I can drive across the bridge to Quebec, go find some all-night poutine place and hash this out over a mountain of fries, cheese curds and gravy."

Alex squeezed her shoulder. "And pulled pork and bacon."

She laughed. "And whatever else the first all-night poutine place we find puts on fries. We'll talk this whole thing out, until I get all this nonsense off my chest and out of my heart, and then after that, maybe we'll decide that I need to back off from this assignment."

It was the conversation she'd been dreading having. But it was a conversation she knew she needed to have. And maybe it would help.

"In the meantime," she added, "let's just focus on the mission for tonight and stop worrying about me. I'm fine."

"No, you're not quite fine, but you will be." Alex's smile was gentle. "I have infinite faith in you."

There was a gentle tap on the window. She turned. Leo was standing outside the van.

Alex leaned past her. "Hey, Leo. You ready to roll?"

"You bet." The commander smiled. "Let's get this over and done with."

Leo took a step back and opened Zoe's door. He was in dress uniform again, the crisp dark lines making him look every bit the very handsome and command-ing hero that he was. No wonder women had bought tickets to tonight's event in the hopes of winning a date with him. She felt his gaze sweep over her from the top of her carefully fluffed hair to the tips of her stiletto shoes, and felt like a teenager on her first date.

Focus on the girls. Focus on Eve and Ivy. She told herself. *Remember that those girls need their father to come home to them safely.*

He reached for her hand. She let him take it and hopped down.

"You look fantastic," he said. "Nobody would ever guess that you're my secret weapon."

She laughed. "Well, that's kind of the point."

"So, you two good to go?" Alex asked.

"Of course," she said. "Yeah, we're good."

She glanced back. Alex was holding out Leo's ear-piece waiting for him to take it and she realized that she and Leo were still holding hands. She pulled away, stepped aside and waited while Alex fitted Leo with an earpiece and cuff link microphone.

"I'm hoping we can keep this job short and simple," Leo said. He adjusted his cuff. "A couple of hours, maybe less. We'll walk in through the service entrance to avoid the press. I'll circulate the room and wait for my contact to approach. Zoe keeps her eyes out for The Anemoi or for any other interference. We go in, we get out, everyone goes home safe. I head up to Cedar Lake to meet up with my girls, taking the intel with me. All good?"

"All good," she said. It was all so simple. Foolproof even. Just a couple short hours and then she'd be wrapping up a job well done and it would be over. She and Leo would say goodbye. And she'd be tucked away in a poutine restaurant with Alex, drowning her heartache in greasy fast food.

"Copy that," Alex said. "I'll be waiting here for you, monitoring your earpieces and the security cams."

Leo looked at her. "Ready?"

To go walk into a fancy gala, hang on his arm and pretend they had the kind of relationship she wanted but could never have? How could anyone ever be ready for that?

Yet, she nodded. "As ready as I'll ever be. I agree, it should be a simple mission."

And she was determined to keep it that way.

They left Alex behind in the van. Their footsteps echoed in the dark empty parking garage. They walked side by side, silently, so close their hands almost touched. They reached the delivery door. Leo eased it open and then held it for her to walk through. Then he covered his microphone.

"You okay?" he whispered.

She looked up at him and smiled. "Yeah, I'm good."

He leaned close. "You know, when I met Samantha she seemed so perfect for Josh. But I still can't imagine Theresa marrying a bodyguard like your brother."

She laughed softly and covered her own microphone in return.

"Josh and Samantha are both analytical introverts," she said. "Don't feel guilty about interrupting the tail end of their honeymoon, because I'm sure there's nothing they'd find more romantic than quietly working on intel together. But Alex and Theresa's relationship is gloriously messy. They're definitely opposites. They joke that she's the brain and he's the brawn. She'll be thrilled to know he's the one tucked safe in the van tonight and I'm the one heading into the party with you."

His smile deepened and warmed something inside her. "I'm glad you're the one heading into the party with me, too."

"Okay, guys." Alex's voice crackled loudly in her ear. "The venue manager has confirmed that the last of the food deliveries came through over an hour ago. Interior hallways are clear. Security is on the door upstairs. You shouldn't run into anyone."

They walked down a long utility hallway. Bare bulbs hung from the ceiling ahead. Pipes ran down the side of the walls. She gave a quick wave to the security camera as they walked past.

"Hey, sis," Alex said. "I see you. When you hit the end of the hallway, turn right and head up three flights of stairs. Then you'll reach a landing. There will be a door to your left."

She smiled under her breath. She could remember as much from the schematics from their planning back at the hotel. Silence pressed around them filled only with the sound of their footsteps, the gentle thrum of the furnace somewhere in the distance and the water gurgling in the pipes. They turned the corner, found the stairs and started climbing.

"I'm sorry this isn't a more glamorous way to make an entrance," Leo said.

"You kidding?" Zoe said. She grinned. "It's a well-known fact that secret entrances like this are what all the cool celebrities use to sneak in and out of places like this."

They reached the first landing. His phone buzzed. Leo raised the phone and frowned.

Her eyes glimpsed the screen.

Sorry I'm going to be a bit late tonight. But very worth it. Big package for you. Have your wallet ready. Killian

Killian Lynch? Since when was he texting Leo?

"What was that about?" she asked. "I'm sorry, I couldn't help but notice that text was from Killian Lynch. I didn't realize you two were on speaking terms."

Leo frowned. "Don't worry about it."

Except he looked really bothered by it and this was Killian they were talking about.

"I am worried about it." Her hand brushed his arm. "He's the same odious, dishonest, despicable blogger who posted those pictures of us that he got from who knows where. I don't like him and I don't trust him."

"You don't have to trust him." His face set. "Just stay out of our way and watch my back if he comes over to talk to me."

Her feet stopped halfway up the staircase. "Please tell me he's not your informant."

"I honestly don't know," Leo said. "Even if I did, I wouldn't be able to confirm it. But if not, he can help me figure out who took those pictures. I've agreed to meet him tonight. He wants to strike some sort of deal. I know we said that the informant could be some white hat, vigilante hacker like Seth Miles, trying to save the military from criminals in its ranks. But that's wishful thinking. He could just as easily be a selfish, media star wanting to make some quick money."

Her hands grabbed the railing and suddenly she realized her arms were shaking. Maybe she'd been a bit of a chicken and not told Leo about what had happened between her and Killian in the past. Maybe she'd hoped he'd stay true to his promise to never search her name online and read her past bad press, and that he could walk out of her life at the end of this mission with his image of her intact and unblemished.

It had never once crossed her mind that Killian could be his informant and the person they'd been trying to connect with all this time. Leo kept walking, like she hadn't even stopped, and she found herself hurrying to keep up with him. They'd reached the final landing. Just one more flight of dingy stairs and they'd reach the ballroom level.

"Wait." Her hand landed on his arm. "I told you, I have a history. When I was a teenager I was kicked off my sports team and suspended from competing for elbowing someone—"

He stopped. "And I told you I don't care about your past—"

"It was Killian Lynch," she said. Leo froze. His

face went carefully blank. She kept talking, quickly. "I know this is really bad timing, that you've been trying for days to meet with your informant. I respect that. But I need you to hear my story. Please."

"Okay," he said. "Talk."

She took a deep breath and let the words come out in a rush.

"Killian was a creep," she said. "It was worse than I let on. He would whisper offensive and gross things in the girls' ears for fun, trying to get a reaction out of us. Subtle stuff to make us feel worthless. My coach told us to hold our heads high and ignore him. But one day, when I was getting ready to compete, he leaned up behind me and whispered something creepy in my ear and something inside me snapped. I spun around with my elbow high and it caught him in the face. I didn't mean to strike him. I just wanted him to back off. I didn't even know the cameras were rolling."

Leo leaned back against the railing. "And that's why you stopped competing?"

"The competition was delayed on the spot," she said. "Can you imagine the chaos of a top male competitor getting a bloody nose from a girl half his size on live television? I was suspended from the team immediately. Killian pushed his case in the press that I didn't deserve to represent my country on the national stage. He said I needed to be taught a lesson. Privately the coach said I was unlikely to make the team again when my suspension was over. So I quit and switched to noncompetitive mixed martial arts. It didn't have the same profile on the national stage. But I preferred it that way."

She felt so stupid and small. How could she have

lost her temper like that and accidentally elbowed someone in the face when the cameras were rolling?

Leo didn't answer. He walked back down to the next landing and somehow she knew that he needed her not to follow him. For a moment she wondered if he was going all the way back to the van. But then he stopped. His hands gripped the railing. His gaze rose up the staircase to the ceiling high above them and she could see him praying under his breath. Then he looked back up at her, with a look so calm and inscrutable it was unnerving.

"Well," he said. "This is unfortunate, hopefully it won't complicate things, if he does indeed turn out to be my informant. If you give me a minute, I'm going to go make a phone call."

"Guys," Alex said. "I'm really sorry to interrupt, but we have someone coming your way and fast."

Even as he spoke, they could hear the footsteps pelting down the hall toward them. She spun around. A man in a tuxedo and shaggy blond hair was barreling down the hallway toward her. It was Jason. She could hear Alex's voice in her ear and Leo yelling something below her. Her hands rose in front of her face.

Jason barreled into her, bodychecking her like a linebacker.

She flew backward down the stairs.

TEN

Leo's heart stopped as he saw Zoe tumble backward down the stairs. She cradled her arms around her head to protect herself as she fell. He ran up the stairs toward her. She hit the landing and groaned.

"Zoe!" He was at her side in a moment. "Are you okay? Are you hurt?"

She pulled herself up onto her hands and knees. "I'm fine."

Leo paused. Jason stood at the top of the stairs, his eyes wide, like he was caught on the knife's edge between fight and flight. Then Jason spun around and pelted down the hall. Leo turned back to Zoe. She'd already grabbed the railing and hauled herself up to her feet. Everything in his heart wanted to stop the mission and hold her. But his mind was shouting that she was his bodyguard, his backup on this mission and his second pair of eyes. Not his to sweep into his arms and hold there. It was time he started acting like it. "Are you sure that you're okay?"

"Yes." She gritted her teeth. "I'll be sore but nothing serious. I've definitely seen worse."

"Okay, good." Leo raised his cuff link microphone

to his mouth. "Alex, Zoe is down. It's a minor fall, but she might need backup. I'm going after Jason."

Then he sprinted up the stairs taking them two at a time, without letting himself look back. Leo ran down the hall. He could see Jason ahead of him, his tall lanky form sprinting down the hallway with the speed and skill of an athlete.

"Zoe!" He could hear Alex in his earpiece. "What's going on? Talk to me. I've got eyes on Leo chasing someone but I can't see you."

"It was Jason." Zoe was panting. "Our fake cop from the parade. He knocked me down a few stairs."

Jason reached the end of a hallway and disappeared around a corner. Leo's footsteps sped up.

"He what?" Alex's voice rose.

"I'm fine!" Zoe said. "I'm a bit sore. Nothing serious."

Alex blew out a hard breath. "Leo left you and went after him alone?"

"Because I'm fine."

Leo rounded the corner and paused. The hallway was empty. Four doors lay ahead in two different directions. He raised his microphone to his mouth. "Alex, I need your help. I've lost him."

"Hang on," Alex said. Leo heard typing. "He cut through the kitchen and entered the ballroom. If you take the second door on your left you should be able to cut him off. It's pretty crowded, but I'll keep scanning for him."

"Got it," Leo said. He slid the door open a crack, looked in and blinked. The grand, sparkling opulence of the ballroom was such a stark difference from the gray, utilitarian ugliness of the hallway it was like opening a portal to another world. The room was huge, with sweeping alcoves and tall pillars, making it impossible to scan the whole room at once. People in tuxedos, gowns and dress uniforms rustled past, seemingly blind to the tiny crack he'd opened between the one world and the next. "I'm about to go in. Once I enter the party I'm going off the mic unless it's urgent."

"Understood," Alex said.

"Commander, do you want me to join you?" Zoe asked. He could hear her running down the hall.

"Negative," Leo said. "The sight lines in here are terrible. I suggest you take a different entrance and scan the room from the other side. The top priority tonight is making contact with Killian. After that, I'll be looking for the informant if it turns out not to be him. Having you by my side will make that harder, and honestly, if I'd realized the kind of past you had with him, I wouldn't have agreed to having you in on this mission. As it is, I think I'd be better off handling this alone. Sorry to change the game plan, but I'm taking this solo. Please keep an eye on the room, but just keep your personal distance. Okay?"

A long pause stretched down the earpiece that seemed to take forever. Then Zoe said, "Understood."

Leo switched off his microphone, straightened his uniform and stepped into the room. Immediately the glamour and buzz of the party enveloped him. Chandeliers glittered above him like stars. A tall dais stood at one end with a microphone and podium. He allowed himself to be swept along by the current of people as he moved through the room, nodding his head to people he knew and to those he didn't, exchanging quick words of small talk and moving on, all while his eyes scanned the crowd. Alex and Zoe had gone silent from his earpiece. But still, the memory of Alex asking Zoe if he'd really just left her there in the staircase and run after Jason pricked like a knife tip against the edges of Leo's heart. He couldn't tell if it was coming from Alex's tone or from Leo's own conscience. Why? If Alex or Josh had fallen down a few stairs, nobody would've thought twice if Leo had gone chasing after a criminal alone. And he could think of at least a dozen strong women he'd served with who'd have expected him to do exactly the same if it had been them—and none of them held a candle to Zoe's strength and grit.

Then why did leaving her there bother him so much?

He kept circling, nodding, smiling and waving off the small, complicated-looking foodstuff that the waitstaff kept offering him. Then a flash of purple caught his eye, making his footsteps stop in their tracks. It was Zoe. She was on the opposite side of the room, her slight and stunning form somehow seeming to stand all alone in the mass of people swirling around her, as if Leo was seeing the entire world through a camera and she was the only thing in focus.

His phone rang. He answered it. "Hello?"

"Hello, Commander Darius! It's Killian Lynch!"

The Irishman's voice boomed down the line, and suddenly Zoe's story filled his mind. Was Killian Lynch really his contact? Was he carrying secret intel about drug smuggling routes? Did he know the identity of who'd had him under surveillance? Leo couldn't see anyone else it could be. Yet the thought of handing over money to someone who'd treated Zoe that way grated something deep inside him. The whole reason that Leo had been brought in to this mission was to be a calm, steady, impartial conduit and bridge. But he'd never dreamed of being in a situation like this.

Guide me, Lord, what do I do? I despise this man for what he did to Zoe. But he could have information that's vital to international security. If I can't set aside my heart for the sake of duty, what kind of man does it make me?

"How's the charity auction going?" Killian asked.

"Fine." Leo's eyes scanned the crowd. "Are you here?"

"No, but I will be soon."

"And you've got something for me?" Leo asked.

"Boy, do I ever," Killian said. "Pulled some pretty big strings and downloaded it from a very private source. Prepare to have your mind blown. By the way, I'm so sorry about that article I published about you and Zoe Dean. I hope you're not offended. I'm just doing my job and did my best to make you look good."

Leo's jaw clenched. All he had to do was get through tonight, be polite and then he could put this whole mess behind him.

"Tell me honestly, though," Killian continued. "Off the record. No spin. Just one guy talking to another. You and Zoe Dean aren't really involved, right? You aren't really dating her?"

His eyes dragged him back to where he'd seen Zoe standing just moments before, but she'd disappeared into the crowd.

"No, Zoe Dean and I are not dating," Leo said. "Not at all. We met at the castle gala and escaped the fire together. She is the friend of a friend of mine, and we've stayed in touch. But that's it and I'd appreciate it if you'd stop harassing us. We are not romantically involved. Please just kill the story."

"Knew it!" Killian's laughter filled the phone, loud and braying. "Listen I've known Zoe from a long way back and I've got her number. I know what kind of person she is—"

"Hang on," Leo cut in. "You might want to check your tone. I'm not saying I don't have a good deal of respect for her—"

"But it's not a romance. Got it. Leave it to me. Consider the story killed."

The phone went dead.

Leo stared at his phone. He'd never heard Killian talk like that, and what made it all the worse was the implication he somehow thought he and Leo were on the same side. His jaw set. No, this would not do.

That settles it, Lord, I can't let this man get away with disrespecting Zoe. I need to have her back. But I can't let Admiral Jacobs down, either. Guide me, please. I need Your wisdom.

He ended his prayer and took a deep breath. He'd done two circuits of the room and was no closer to finding Jason or anyone else in The Anemoi. Or in being approached by anyone else who could be his informant. He'd probably played it alone for too long and needed to reconnect with Zoe and Alex. He'd made a knee-jerk reaction to take it solo that he was already beginning to regret. He stepped back into the relative privacy of the wall, activated his microphone link and held his phone to his mouth as cover. "Zoe? Can we meet by the dessert table in five? I think we need to regroup."

But any answer Zoe gave was suddenly swallowed up by the sound of people clapping as a loud wave of applause swept over the room. Nigel had stepped up to the podium. He welcomed the crowd and launched into his opening jokes. Leo slid his phone back into his pocket and waited.

"I especially want to thank our very special guest Commander Leo Darius." Nigel yanked his attention up to the stage. "Leo, please come to the stage!"

Okay, and what was this? Leo forced a smile on his face, pushed off the wall and walked up to the front of the room, nodding, smiling and shaking hands as he went. He mounted the dais and joined Nigel at the podium.

"What is this?" he whispered.

"A solution to the problem you've put me in," Nigel said. The smile on his mouth didn't come anywhere near meeting his eyes. He turned back to the microphone. "Now, as you know, Leo had originally promised to take someone to the theater followed by a private dinner at one of Ottawa's top restaurants. I know a lot of you bought tickets to tonight's event based on hearing that in the press and I can tell you, we've never had attention like that before in the history of these events. Online bids have been coming in from all over the country. So, I'm very sorry to tell you that sadly, Leo called me last night to say that due to personal issues he'd no longer be able to fulfill this promise."

Some light booing rose from the crowd. It was mostly good-natured, and even mingled with laughter, but it did nothing to stem the feel of a threat at the back of Leo's neck. Had he been wrong all this time?

Had Nigel been behind this? Even part of this? Leo's smile grew tighter. Whether Nigel was part of The Anemoi or not, he was playing right into their hands and increasing the possibility of them reaching the informant before he did.

"So, we've decided to arrange a little surprise for the commander!" Nigel said.

Leo's face froze. What was Nigel trying to do? Admiral Jacobs's warning to stay natural and not do anything to tip anyone off floated through the back of his mind. But the stakes were growing higher. This was his last opportunity to retrieve the intel. He couldn't let Nigel ruin that.

"What's going on?" Zoe's voice crackled in his ear. "We weren't briefed on this."

He had no idea. As Nigel rambled on about Leo's prestigious military history, two waitstaff stepped on stage behind them, and set up a small café table and two chairs. They set the table with military efficiency, lit candles and poured sparkling punch into long, tall flutes. Leo's stomach sank.

"This is your opportunity to bid on a special, private dinner date with Commander Darius, here at this event," Nigel said. "For the next two hours, you and Leo can share an intimate meal and conversation, up here on the dais, waited on by staff, with special desserts and food."

"We have to stop this," Zoe said. "If he's stuck up on that dais all night, he won't be able to do the handoff."

"Well, he'd better come up with a very good reason," Alex said, "and fast. Because walking off the dais looks like a pretty bad option from where I'm sitting, but getting stuck up there isn't any better."

Alex wasn't wrong. If he walked off the dais he'd cause a scene and tip off whoever was watching him that something was wrong. But if he went through with the auction date, he'd lose his opportunity for the handoff.

"Who'll start the bidding at one hundred dollars?" Nigel said.

Hands shot up. The room was filled with good-natured laughter. Cameras started clicking. In seconds the bidding was up to three hundred dollars.

"What do we do?" It was Zoe.

"We leave it," Alex said. "Leo wanted to go solo. He can handle this on his own. Maybe we should let this play out."

"Six hundred and fifty dollars," Nigel called. "Going once."

The room spun. Were they really going to leave him up there on his own, torn with two bad options, between being sidelined and sitting on a stage for the rest of the night, or causing a scene?

"He hired us to watch his back," Zoe said.

"Going twice," Nigel said.

"Then he changed the game plan and decided to go it alone," Alex said. "He changed the parameters. Not us."

"Well, it looks like that's all the bids we got, folks." Nigel's gavel rose. "Looks like the privilege of an evening, an hour alone—"

"Two thousand, four hundred and twenty-eight dollars and sixteen cents!" Zoe's voice rose above the crowd. The gavel froze. There she stood, in the middle of the ballroom, facing the dais, like a fighter entering the circle, daring anyone to challenge her.

Nigel's jaw dropped.

"Thank you," Leo whispered.

He watched as her lips moved and her voice brushed his ear. "You're welcome. I knew you wanted to get out of there."

Murmurs rose from the crowd, their voices blending into white noise.

"Is that all the money you've got," he asked softly.

"Yeah." She smiled. "Why wear yourself out deflecting a lot of little blows, when you can go for a single knockout punch?"

"Well, that's a pretty big jump in bidding!" Nigel's laugh rang loud and hollow. "Does anyone want to bid us up to a nice round two thousand five hundred?"

Leo reached for the gavel and pulled it smoothly from Nigel's hand.

"I think we should stop there, don't you, Nigel?" He leaned into the microphone and swirled the gavel through his fingers like a weapon. A wide smile crossed his face for the benefit of the crowd. "That was my date for the night, Zoe Dean, bidding there. I'm happy to donate the extra myself to round it up. But I'm afraid it would be awfully rude of me to invite a woman to an event like this and then sit with someone else for the entire night, don't you think?"

"Well, I guess I can't argue with that," Nigel said. He looked genuinely confused and for a moment Leo wondered if it really had been no more than a foolish misunderstanding. "Thank you again, Commander Leo, for your very generous support!"

"I'm going to go to the bidding booth at the front desk and settle up," Zoe said, in his ear.

"Zooooooeeeeeee…" Alex said his sister's name like it had six syllables.

"Don't start with me, Alex. Also, you're paying for poutine."

The voices in his earpiece were drowned out by clapping. Zoe disappeared back into the crowd, and he lost sight of her. But Leo lingered on the stage, long enough to take photos with Nigel, and then a handful of fans who were disappointed to have been outbid. But he barely noticed them as they flitted around him like lightning bugs. He knew what it was like to have someone admire him, adore him even, without ever seeing the person inside. It was a shallow empty feeling. He'd had that with Marisa when her youthful crush on the man she'd hoped he was faded into an aching emptiness when she hadn't fallen for the man inside his protective shell.

But Zoe knew him. She saw him. And while he was sure that between Ash Private Security and his own bank account they'd find a way to make her whole again, she was still willing to empty out everything she had, just to have his back.

A sudden shout filled his ear, so loudly it was if Zoe was standing right behind him.

"What? No! Stop!" Zoe was shouting. "Get your hands off me!"

Where was she? What was happening?

He excused himself from the stage and pushed through the crowd. A cacophony of noises filled his earpiece. Male voices were barking orders. Zoe was protesting. Alex was scrambling in vain to figure out where she was.

"Zoe what's happening?" Leo's step quickened through the crowd. He exited the banquet hall, ran down the stairs and reached the front entrance. The bidding table was empty except for two young, shell-shocked volunteers. He wheeled around and raised the cuff to his mouth. "Alex! Where is she?"

"Outside." Alex's voice filled his ear. "Two men are dragging her out."

Zoe's stilettos scuffed on the stone steps as two large security guards tried to aggressively escort her from the building. One was in her face. The other was trying to handcuff her wrists behind her back. She could hear Alex and Leo shouting in her ear, but couldn't get her microphone anywhere near her face to answer. She could see the flash of press cameras in her face, feel the glare of television cameras and hear the babble of reporters shouting questions from behind the velvet rope. Shame washed over her as potential headlines filled her eyes.

Disgraced Gymnast Zoe Dean Dragged Out of Charity Auction in Handcuffs, would be the kind of headline they'd run if she didn't fight back. Bam! Crash! Pow! Disgraced Gymnast Zoe Dean in Violent Struggle with Security Guards! would be the headline if she did.

She couldn't let herself fight them. Not on assignment. Not in front of the press. She felt the cold metal of handcuffs clicking over her wrists.

"What's the meaning of this?" Leo's voice boomed through the night air. He strode out the front door with an authority and strength that took her breath away. "Could somebody please explain what you're doing manhandling my date?"

The security guards stopped, pushing her to the side almost as an afterthought as they turned to face him.

"I'm sorry, but she didn't have an invitation on her and wasn't on the guest list," the larger, more burly security man spoke. His chest puffed out. But even in the darkness, Zoe could tell his face was reddening.

"Take her handcuffs off," Leo said. "Now."

It wasn't a request. It was an order. Zoe felt the younger of the two security guards removing the cuffs from her wrists, a lot more gently than his partner had put them on. But the other security guard still wasn't backing down.

"With all due respect, we got a tip that this woman wasn't your date," he spluttered. "In fact, we were told she was a menace who was stalking you, and that you'd asked her to leave you alone. We were told you wanted her removed from the premises."

Fire burned in the depth of Leo's eyes. "Who told you that?"

The larger guard shook his head and didn't answer. But the younger guard pointed toward the bottom of the stairs. They turned. Killian Lynch was walking up the stairs toward them, his smile smug and his eyes malicious. The media man waved a hand at the security guards.

"Guys, we're good. Sorry, sorry. False alarm. So sorry for wasting your time." Killian raised both hands palm up and shrugged at Leo. "Guess I must've misunderstood when you told me you weren't involved with Miss Dean and didn't want anything to do with her. I just thought I needed to teach Miss Dean a bit of a lesson."

She's out of control. Someone needs to teach her a lesson.

Just like that the world froze in tableau around Zoe. The security guards were trying to shrink back up the stairs behind her. Alex was in her ear, offering to run all the way from the parking garage, up three flights of stairs, to the front of the building to grab Killian by the scruff of the neck and haul him away from his sister.

Leo stood in front of her, strong and supportive like her champion, with his hand outstretched to help her and fight for her. She took a deep breath and felt a prayer fill her heart. She'd spent almost fifteen years beating herself up for one moment of losing self-control in front of an international audience and elbowing Killian in the face. She'd punished herself for that moment long enough.

She needed to forgive herself.

"Zoe," Leo spoke her name as his hand brushed her shoulder and the world started moving again. "Are you okay?"

"No." She took his hand and squeezed it hard. "But I will be."

This was her fight. Not his. She dropped Leo's hand and walked down the stairs toward Killian. He met her halfway up the stairs. They stood there for a moment, eye to eye, her feet one step above his.

"Have you learned your lesson yet?" Killian asked.

"Yes, I have." Her chin lifted. "Not whatever lesson you thought you were trying to teach me. But the lesson I needed to learn. I learned that I'm going to make mistakes and I'm going to mess up, so I need to get better at forgiving myself and at accepting forgiveness where it's offered."

He spluttered like steam was boiling under his skin and it was choking his ability to speak. And for the first time she looked him directly in the face. He was older than she remembered. It was like he'd been frozen in her mind as a picture all these years and it was her first time seeing just how much older he'd gotten. Light from the hotel entrance fell over his face and she saw the dent in the bridge of his nose. Clarity broke over her like sunshine. Her hand rose to her lips.

"I broke your nose," she said. "I'm so sorry. I had no idea."

"If you ever say that to anyone I will destroy you." Killian's face went red. "You think I'd let some small, pathetic nothing of a girl break my nose?"

Yes, he had. She knew it without a shadow of a doubt. Memories rushed back from that moment, filling her mind. She remembered the crack she'd heard when she accidentally struck him, the way he'd grabbed his face and swore, and the way his nose had bled. She remembered how he'd disappeared from the rest of the competition and been so determined to destroy her and make sure she never competed again. Above all, she could see it in his eyes right now, despite the denying lies on his lips. He had never been able to let it go and was still so furious all these years later and determined to make her pay.

"I'm sorry I broke your nose," she said. "I apologize. I didn't mean to hit you and honestly had no idea I'd struck you that hard."

Killian's face grew even redder. "You're apologizing to me?"

"Yes." She was. It was time. She needed to. "I'm not apologizing for telling you to back off and leave me alone, back then. You were a creep, and you were totally out of line. I was right to defend myself. But I didn't know my own strength. I didn't check how close the physical distance was between us. I was sloppy and undisciplined, and still had a lot to learn about combat fighting. And, yes, I am truly sorry."

Killian stepped up onto the step beside her, until they stood toe to toe. He leaned close, his breath heavy with anger and alcohol. "Do you actually think I'm ever going to forgive you?"

"No, I don't," she said. "I hope you do, for your sake. But even if you don't, I'm going to let it go."

His hand jabbed into his jacket pocket and yanked it out again so quickly she flinched. There was an envelope in his hand, plain white, with Leo's name written on it.

"See this, Leo?" Killian waved it over her head. "I told you that I had something for you and I wasn't kidding. I thought maybe we could work out some kind of arrangement to keep this from ever getting leaked to the tabloids. But you have the worst taste in women."

Zoe took a long, hard look at the man she'd been frightened of all these years and shook her head. Then she turned to Leo. "I'm done here. I'll see you inside."

She started up the stairs. But Killian leaped up two more steps and got in front of her.

"You think you can just walk away from me?" Killian stood over her. "You think this is over?"

He lunged forward for her arm. She waited until she felt his fingertips touch her skin then she leaped to the side with precision. He pitched forward, lost his bal-

ance and fell, sprawling down the stairs on his hands
and knees. Faint laughter rippled through the crowd of
reporters below. Killian sprang to his feet. Hate filled
his eyes. He ran at her, throwing the old vile names he
used to call girls like her in secret, loudly and openly
like fireworks exploding around them.

"How dare you!" He charged at her. His arm rose
to slap Zoe across the face. But before his blow could
land, Leo stepped in between them, so that Killian's
strike just ended up smacking Leo's strong chest, before ineffectually bouncing off again.

"Back off." Leo's arms crossed. "You're making a
fool out of yourself."

"She pushed me down the stairs!"

"No, she didn't," Leo said. "She just got out of your
way when you tried to lay a hand on her and you face-
planted. Then you hit me. Both of which were no doubt
caught by the security cameras and the host of pho-
tographers you decided to pull your stunt in front of.
Diplomatic immunity doesn't protect you from looking like a fool."

Killian's fist shot out again, aimed straight at Leo's
jaw. The commander dodged the blow, then caught the
man's fist before he could yank it back.

"You're done," Leo said. "Stop before you make an
even bigger fool of yourself."

"Your life is over." Killian swore. He yanked his
hand back, pulled his phone from his pocket and
pushed a button. Then he waved his envelope in Leo's
face again. "You have no idea how bad it's going to
get. Or what you're going to lose. I've just posted the
contents of this envelope online. I was going to give
you the opportunity to buy this from me. But now it's

too late, and I'm just going to sit back and enjoy watching as your life is ruined."

Leo didn't even flinch. He reached down and yanked the white envelope from Killian's hand without saying a word. Then he slid his arm around Zoe's shoulders and led her back up the stairs. She could hear Alex applauding in her earpiece. Leo leaned his head against hers, pulling her close into his side as they reentered the hotel.

"I'm sorry about that," Leo said. "This whole situation is a joke. As much as part of me hopes this envelope really does contain the intel I'm after, so that this will all finally be over, I can't actually believe that all our hard work could come down to this nonsense. I thought whoever my informant was, and whatever they were bringing me, it was a matter of vital security. Not whatever colossal waste of time this has turned out to be. Now, if this is indeed my intel and that creep was really my informant, all I can do is analyze it, let the right person in military intelligence know about this and let them handle it. What a mess."

His hand slipped from her shoulder. He pulled the paper out of the envelope and scanned the page. Then, as she watched, the color drained from his face. His eyes closed.

"What's wrong? Leo, talk to me?"

"This isn't about military secrets or smuggling. This is something far worse." He opened his eyes, and it was as if someone had emptied them of their light. He raised the cuff link microphone to his mouth, and she realized his hand was shaking. "Alex, I need to talk to Zoe about something and it needs to be private. Can you do me a favor and find us a private location?"

"No problem," Alex said.

"Thank you," Leo said. He took her hand and held it like she was the only thing keeping him from falling. "I hate to ask this, but I'm going to need to ask you to cut audio feed, too. I need to talk to Zoe alone."

ELEVEN

Zoe's heart ached as she watched the color drain from Leo's face. *Lord, what could Killian possibly have to extort anyone with to make him so upset?*

"There's a rose garden down the hallway to your left," Alex said. "Good lines of sight but very private. I haven't seen Jason or any other Anemoi operatives since the stairwell, but I'll keep scanning."

"Thank you." Leo led her down a hallway and through a pair of double doors. They stepped back out into the muggy night. The sound of the Ottawa river roared in the distance. Leo led her through a maze of towering rosebushes over to a bench by the fountain. They sat.

"Okay, guys," Alex said. "I'm cutting the audio. But I'm going to turn it back on if anyone approaches you or if either of you wave at the camera. And I'm maintaining visual."

The hiss in her ear went silent. Leo turned to her on the bench. He took both of her hands in his.

"First of all, I'm sorry," he said. "I had no idea Killian was such a creep. I've been completely focused on my mission and when he said he had something to sell me, I just assumed they might possibly be connected. I was wrong. Killian is not our guy and this is not my intel. I never realized he'd seen us together and was out for revenge. If I had, I wouldn't have put you in a position where there was even the possibility he could hurt you."

But if the envelope didn't contain the intel then what had Leo so rattled?

"It's okay," she said.

"No, it's not. I should've had your back." His thumb stroked over her fingers, and then he let go of her hand, pulled out the paper and folded it carefully, so that just two blocks of text filled the screen. "Marisa was a very private person but she kept a diary on her computer. When she died, I erased her computer and donated it to a charity store. I knew she hadn't been happy in our marriage. I knew she'd asked for separation and had considered divorce. I just wanted that sad chapter of my life to be over and didn't want to read it. Apparently somebody got their hands on it and was able to retrieve a letter that Marisa had written to me. I can only guess that Killian was going to use it to blackmail me. But after seeing us together, he's posted it online."

He handed her the paper. She read.

"… I'm sorry you never got to meet Melody. She is the most caring and compassionate woman I've ever met and like a second mother to them. It is my dying wish that the girls go live with her, and for Melody to have custody of them.

"I don't know how to say this, Leo, but I'm sorry, you are not the girls' father. I'm sorry I didn't have the courage to tell you this when I was alive. I had a relationship with another man who did not want to marry me when I told him about Ivy or to acknowledge Eve when she was conceived. I was wrong to use you this way. I was a coward to marry you, knowing that I did not love you. You weren't a good husband and you were a bad father. I wish I'd never involved you in our lives.

"Whether she realizes it or not, Melody knows the identity of the girls' real father and how to contact him. Hopefully he will change his mind about being in their lives. I know that she will do everything in her power to find him and to be a good mother to them. You promised me that you wouldn't have another romantic relationship until the girls were grown. I asked you that because I wanted to protect them, so that you couldn't make the same mistake I did. Now I think it is best if you relinquish custody of the girls and let them go on with their lives without you."

The letter continued onto the next page, but Zoe didn't need to read it. She'd read enough.

"Before you ask," Leo said, "there are other parts of this letter that contain information only Marisa could've known. I have no doubt that she wrote those parts and that they were saved on her laptop. Melody is a friend of Marisa's. We talked on the phone last night about arranging a playdate with her sons. But I don't know what to think about the rest of this. I just don't. I knew Marisa wasn't happy..."

His voice trailed off. She reached for his hands again and pried the paper from his grasp as she linked her fingers through his.

"Leo, look at me, please," she said softly. His eyes met hers. The depth of worry etched there made pain fill her own chest so sharply that tears slipped from her eyes and slid down her cheeks, as if her heart was breaking for his.

"Other parts of the letter might be true, but not this," she said. "Not this. You are an amazing father to those girls. They love you. They need you. The idea they'd be better off without you is nothing but a cruel lie."

"But what if it's true that I'm not really their father?" he asked. Emotion rumbled in his voice, like the ground before an earthquake. His fingers brushed her cheeks and her tears fell into his palms.

"Did Marisa ever give you reason to doubt her?" she asked.

"No, but that doesn't mean it's not possible. Whether this letter is a lie or not, I can't ignore it. I can't just stare straight ahead, go on with my life and pretend it's not out there. Not with the damage it could do to my girls." He leaned forward until his forehead rested against hers.

It was hopeless. Killian was headed back to the United Kingdom within hours. Leo imagined he was too smart to leave online proof that he'd posted the letter himself. Even if police questioned Killian about how he'd gotten ahold of Marisa's letter and who'd sent him the aerial drone photos, they wouldn't be able to hold him indefinitely and there was nothing to stop him from skipping the country. Even if there was, the damage was done, the letter was out there, the story would be spread, questions would be asked and those little girls' lives would be irrevocably changed by it.

He'd tried so hard to protect them. Finally something had struck he couldn't protect them from.

"No matter what happens next, the girls know you love them," she said. "They know you're going to be there for them. They know you will protect them and that they were so blessed to be loved by you."

Her eyes closed as her words failed. He held her there for a long moment. Then she felt his mouth brush against her cheeks, kissing the tears from her skin. She tilted her face up toward him. His lips met hers. He kissed her, allowing their lips to meet for one sweet and tender moment. Then he pulled her into his arms and he hugged her.

"Thank you," he said. "Thank you for being here. Thank you for everything. I have to leave. I promised the girls that I'd be there in the morning and now it's even more important that I'm there. Thankfully we'll be cut off from the world for a few days at the cottage, which will give me time to think, pray and get advice on how to handle this. I failed in my mission. The gala will be wrapping up any moment now, if it hasn't already. I never met the informant and got the data, and with the delegates heading home tomorrow it looks like I never will. All I know is that I need to go be with my daughters. Protecting them is the only thing that matters now."

"I understand," she said.

He stood slowly. But his eyes still hadn't left her face, and it was like for the first time she was looking through his protective shield to the man who lay inside. "I can't have any outside distractions right now. Not with the mess that the tabloids are going to stir up in my life. Any outside relationships I have are just going to get caught up in that."

A clock started to ring, the long, deep gongs sounding from somewhere inside the hotel. She stood up slowly and ran her hands down over her party dress. The weeklong symposium was over. The mission was a failure. The glittering, golden fantasy of the life she could have had with an extraordinary man like Leo faded into the mist. Now it was time to sit with her brother in a diner and poke at a mound of fries, cheese curds and gravy with a little wooden notched stick that was masquerading as a fork.

It was time to say goodbye. It was clear from the look in his eyes that he cared for her, and there was no way she was able to hide that she cared about him. The connection they'd both been trying to deny was now lying out there between them. Along with the knowledge there was nothing they could do about it.

"Let's go talk to Alex," she said. "I think we can wrap up this mission pretty quickly and then you can go be with your girls. Josh will finalize things when you see him."

"Thank you," Leo said. His hand reached out as if to touch her shoulder, but then he changed his mind and pulled it back. "Thank you, Zoe Dean. For everything."

She swallowed hard. "You're welcome."

She reached for her ear, switched on her earpiece and raised the bracelet microphone to her lips. "Hey, Alex, we're headed your way—"

A cacophony of gunfire hit her ears. Fear washed

over her body, sending adrenaline pumping through her veins.

"Zoe! Help!" Her brother's voice filled her ears. "I'm under attack!"

Leo ran for the door. Zoe was two steps ahead of him. He yanked a phone from his pocket, dialing 9-1-1 as he ran. Zoe burst through the door to the staircase, then paused, holding the door open as Leo ran down the hall toward her.

"Go! Don't wait for me!" he shouted. He waved at her with one hand and held the phone to his ear with the other. "I'm calling the police, and I'm right behind you. Go save your brother!"

Gratitude filled her eyes. She turned and disappeared down the stairs, taking them two at a time.

"Nine-one-one, emergency services," said a male voice in his ear.

"We need police and ambulance." He forced his footsteps to slow long enough to get the words out clearly as he rattled off the location and address. "There's gunfire in the third level of the underground parking garage."

"Emergency services have been dispatched to your location," the dispatcher said. "Any injuries?"

"I don't know. I don't know how many people are involved, either. Just that my friend is under fire." Judging by what he'd seen of the security guards, he didn't think they'd be likely to leap into a firefight.

"Please remain calm, sir, and get yourself to safety."

That was not going to happen. Zoe was already at the bottom of the staircase and heading into the parking garage.

"Thank you. I've got to go." He dropped his phone into his pocket and kept running down the stairs, vaulting over the final railing and letting his body drop onto the ground below. He reached the door, ten paces behind Zoe, and froze.

Zoe stood, her limbs still quivering with exertion. Alex was down on the ground, pinned on his back, blood pouring from a gunshot wound in his shoulder. Prometheus kneeled over him, a gun in his hand.

Prometheus pressed the barrel against Alex's forehead, right between the eyes.

"Stop right there!" Prometheus barked. "Now! Or I'm going to kill him."

Leo pressed his back against the door frame. He could hear a sob of fear mingling with prayer slipping from Zoe's lips. His chest ached at the sound.

"Get down on your knees, girlie, and put your hands way up where I can see them!" Prometheus ordered. The gun pressed deeper into Alex's forehead. "How many more of you are there? Are you alone?"

"Yes!" Zoe crouched. Her hands stretched up above her head. "It's just me."

She hadn't realized he'd arrived behind her. But more important, neither had Prometheus. The thug had no idea Leo was there, standing in the shelter of the doorway just a foot outside the garage. Emergency sirens echoed from somewhere in the distance. The police were almost there. For a moment it was like the world had frozen into a picture through the archway of the door. Up to this point he'd had no choice in what he'd done. There'd been no other options. His admiral had needed him to intercept the data. Zoe had needed him to leap from the float and rush her to safety.

But now, a cold hard choice lay in front of him. It would take so little to retreat into safety, to walk away from this life of danger and chaos that put his daughters' lives at risk. All he had to do was take one step backward, let the door close behind him and wait. The mission to retrieve the intel was a failure. His backup private security had been captured. His daughters' lives had been plunged into turmoil. Zoe had opened up broken and injured parts of his heart and made them beat painfully, wanting things that couldn't be. But he could still choose to close the door and retreat back into safety, like he'd retreated into quiet failure before.

"Let Alex go," Zoe called. She stood up again slowly and started toward Prometheus. "Take me instead!"

"No!" Leo burst through the door. Prometheus's eyes cut to his face, as he stepped forward into the parking garage behind Zoe. "Don't hurt her. I'm the one you want."

Leo's hands rose. He walked toward Zoe until he was standing just one step behind her. Her eyes were locked on where her brother, Alex, was down on the ground, bleeding and in pain. But as Leo watched, Alex tore his eyes away from the thug, who now pressed him against the ground, and instead he looked at his sister. Alex's lips moved, but Leo couldn't catch what he was saying. Prometheus's eyes flickered from Zoe to Leo and then back to Alex. But still the gun didn't move from Alex's face.

Zoe took another step forward. "Didn't you hear me, Prometheus? That's your handle, right? You're with The Anemoi. I've been watching you from the beginning, stalking you, waiting to see what you wanted to steal. You tried to kidnap me at the parade yesterday. Well, now you can have me. Let my brother go."

"No, take me." Leo's voice rose. "I'm what this has all been about from the beginning, aren't I?"

"They don't want to kill you, Leo." Zoe shook her head. "They want to destroy you. They want to hurt you. Right, Prometheus? That's what your client hired you for, right? Not to steal military secrets but to tear Leo's life apart. If you really want to hurt him, you'll take me."

"Zoe." Leo's voice dropped. "Please, I can't let you do this."

"Trust me, Leo," Zoe said softly, her voice barely a whisper. "I trust you."

Prometheus hesitated, his eyes darted from Zoe to Leo, then back to Alex. Then his eyes locked on Zoe's face.

"You! Girlie! Hands on your head." Prometheus sat back. Zoe folded her hands and set them on top of her head. Prometheus gestured to her with the gun and waved it toward the looming shape of a car in the darkness. "You're coming with me."

TWELVE

Zoe watched as the barrel of the gun moved away from Alex's face. A prayer brushed her lips, as she remembered the words Alex had mouthed to her, "Distract him." Alex's good arm shot up, grabbing Prometheus by the wrist and yanking the gun from his grasp. The weapon clattered into the darkness. Zoe ran for it. Prometheus swore. With one large hand he slammed Alex back against the concrete. The other one rose, ready to pound her injured brother. But he never got the opportunity.

With a roar, Leo leaped, yanking Prometheus off Alex before the blow could fall. The criminal swung back hard, pelting Leo with fast, furious punches. But it was all in vain. Leo stood between Prometheus and her brother, deflecting the blows with a precision and skill that amazed her. Prometheus fell back and then bent down. When he rose back up, a knife flashed in his hand.

"Leo!" Zoe tossed him the gun. "Catch!"

He caught it and spun toward the criminal.

"Drop the knife and get down!" Leo ordered. "Stay down. It's over."

Police sirens filled the air. Flashing lights and head-lights of emergency services poured into the parking garage. Zoe dropped to her knees beside her brother, still curled on the ground. "Alex!"

"Hey, sis." He looked up at her and grinned through gritted teeth. "Nice timing. Great distraction. But I think I'm going to need a rain check on that poutine."

There was a grunt in the darkness. Prometheus wriggled backward across the pavement and turned to run, in one final, desperate attempt to escape capture. Leo grabbed him from behind and yanked him back. Alex and Zoe watched as Leo subdued The Anemoi operative in a simple but effective hold and marched him over to police.

"That was some really impressive teamwork back there," Alex said. "I know we already have one ex-military member of our team. But if Leo's ever look-ing for a change of career, I'm sure Josh would love having a second."

"Leo's mission is over," she said. "The informant never approached him. The whole thing is a bust."

Alex's face went even paler. "I'm sorry."

"Me, too." Zoe stood back and let the paramedics see to her brother, while she went and gave her state-ment to police. By the time she was finished, Alex was sitting on a stretcher in the back of the ambulance and talking with Leo. At some point in the chaos, the com-mander had changed out of his dress uniform and into a simple T-shirt and jeans. As she walked over to join them, Leo left the ambulance and walked toward her.

"Your brother is going to be okay," Leo said. "Nice clean through and through. No permanent damage."

Zoe nodded. "He's tough."

"Like his sister," Leo said. A peculiar warmth seemed to spread between them in the cold, dark garage. "Thankfully, Prometheus has been arrested. Now it's up to police detectives to question him and find out what The Anemoi was after. But as the symposium is done, the informant never identified themselves and our opportunity to get the military data is lost, they shouldn't have any reason to go after me."

She wasn't sure if he was trying to convince her or himself. "Hopefully."

He took a step back, like he was about to back his way across the garage to his truck until he faded into the darkness.

"Look," she said quickly. "I don't believe this was ever just about the smuggling intel."

"That's not logical." He frowned. "None of this happened until the informant contacted Admiral Jacobs and said he had military data to sell."

"Or none of this happened until your face was all over the media," she said. "Look, I know you don't agree with me. But if this is goodbye then I'm going to say my piece. Because if I don't, and something ever happened to you and your amazing daughters, I'd never be able to forgive myself. I think whoever hired The Anemoi wanted to destroy you. I think they saw this strong, handsome, amazing father and hero flash across their media and decided they had to ruin your life. That's why they vandalized the poster of you and went after me. That's why I still believe they're behind that letter from Marisa about your daughters."

Leo grabbed both her hands and held them. "But that goes against everything you've told me about The

Anemoi. They're thieves. They're vigilantes. They don't just torch lives."

"Unless they plan to steal something from the ashes."

"Zoe, I don't have anything left to steal." A long, heavy pause spread to the edges of the darkness. Sadness filled the space between them and everything in her ached to slide her arms around him. Then he took another step backward. "I'm sorry. I've got to go. It's only a few hours until the sun comes up, and the cottage is four hours' drive away."

"I know," she said. "I'll call Josh and Samantha and let them know you're on your way. With your permission, I'll also fill them in on the bombshell about to hit your life. Samantha will be able to find you a lawyer, a damage control consultant and someone who can do a discreet DNA test. She might even figure out a way to find out if Marisa really wrote that letter. It won't stop the tsunami, but should be able to give you a bit of shelter as you figure out how to ride out the storm."

"I'd appreciate that. Thank you." They stood there, their feet just inches away from each other. Then he pulled her into a hug. For one quick moment she felt his arms around her back and the smell of him filled her senses as she heard the sound of his heartbeat against hers. Then he pulled away. She let go. He turned around and walked through the parking garage without looking back. Every step he took seemed to echo around her, creating tiny fissures in the tissue of her heart.

Lord, please help Leo. Give him what he needs. Protect his girls.

He disappeared into the darkness. She turned,

walked toward the ambulance and hopped up onto the back.

Alex sat up and looked at her. "What are you doing here?"

"What do you mean, what am I doing here?" She sat down on a seat in the back of the ambulance. The engine hummed gently. "I'm escorting my brother to the hospital. Because in case you missed it, you've just been shot."

She expected at least a smile from that. But instead Alex rolled his eyes.

"Look, we really don't have time for this," Alex said. "Leo told me about that unbelievably horrible letter from his late wife. And I'm in way too much pain to argue coherently so why don't we just skip ahead to the part where you realize you're wrong, thank me for being awesome, jump out of the ambulance and go running after Leo."

A paramedic climbed into the back and reached to close the door.

"Wait!" Alex held up his one good hand. His phone was clenched between his fingers and she realized he'd been texting. "Hold on. Just give me a second to convince my sister that coming with me would be the biggest mistake of her life."

"Are you insane?" Zoe asked. "You've been shot—"

"Yep!" Alex said. "I've been shot. By a villainous bad guy. A nice clean shot through the shoulder that thankfully won't cause any permanent damage, but will leave me with a very dashing scar. It hurts a whole lot. I really don't recommend it."

Shot or not, he was the same old Alex.

"And you need me." She crossed her arms. "I'm coming to the hospital."

"Theresa is already on her way with Mom and Dad. They'll get there by the time I'm in Recovery. I already texted Samantha and Josh everything on that list you just rattled off to Leo. They're on it." He dropped the phone and reached out toward her. "Don't get me wrong, Zoe, you're the absolute best. But Leo needs you more than I do. If you let him drive off into the night right now, to face what he's going through alone, you're never going to forgive yourself."

Something inside her bristled. "He doesn't need me."

"Come on, Zoe!" Alex groaned. "I told you I don't have time to argue about this! How many times has one of us run right into danger just because another one of us said go? When Josh found Samantha lying on a bomb on the Ash's front porch, you and I didn't stand around and debate what he told us to do. When a crook tried to kill Theresa at Cedar Lake, I didn't doubt your ability to subdue a criminal so that I could go after her. This is what we do. We trust each other and leap into action."

"Not on things like this!"

The paramedic was back again.

"Hang on!" Alex called. "My sister needs one more minute to realize the obvious."

Zoe's eyes shot daggers at him. The moment he was healed and back to being able to train with her, she was going to beat him so hard in a round on the boxing mats.

"One question, sis, and then I won't say another word."

"Fine."

"Why do Theresa and I work together?" Alex asked.

Josh and Samantha are both analytical introverts...but Alex and Theresa's relationship is gloriously messy. They're definitely opposites.

"She's the brains," Zoe said. "You're the brawn."

"Yeah." Alex nodded. "And with Leo, you're the heart. Don't you get that? You're the passion. You're the fire. He's the ice. You're the flames."

"I know! And that's the problem!"

"No, that's the solution." Alex squeezed her hand hard. "You think he's going to survive the fight to save his children on logic alone? He needs emotion. He needs fire. He needs to fight for those girls. He's not going to survive without you. He needs to be with you right now and you need to be with him."

Leo gripped the steering wheel at exactly ten and two. He pulled his truck through the maze of emergency vehicles, up the ramp and out of the parking garage. Dark night air swamped around him. The street was lit in the eerie glow of streetlights. His phone buzzed. He paused at the entrance of the parking garage and checked his messages. There was only one, from Admiral Jacobs. The admiral was out of surgery, doing well and looking forward to hearing from Leo when he could check in.

Thank You, God, for that! But what do I tell him? That I never met up with the informant? That I don't have the intel? And that now I'm going to need to take a leave of absence while I sort out the mess my family is in?

He pulled out onto the empty Ottawa street and

started driving. The clock on his dash read quarter to two. He'd get there before sunup, join the girls for breakfast, and then...

Then what? How could he begin to explain to them what was going on? The sting of knowing his mission had been a failure was nothing compared to knowing what kind of pain this type of gossip could put his girls through.

Help me, Lord. This storm I'm in is so strong and wild—and I feel like I'm in danger of being swept away.

A stop sign loomed ahead, as a flash of red in the glare of his headlights. He tapped his brakes.

"Stop!" A cry sounded in the darkness as a figure leaped in front of his truck. Two hands landed hard on the hood of his truck. He stared through the windshield. It was Zoe—wild, determined and bracing her hands on his hood as if she alone was capable of keeping his truck from moving. She ran around to the passenger door, he unlocked it and she tumbled inside. She buckled the seat belt but was panting so hard she could barely manage more than a single word. "Drive."

He drove, easing the truck through the downtown core toward the highway.

"I was afraid I wouldn't catch you," Zoe said after a long moment. She gasped a breath. "I ran up three flights of stairs, came out the front door and raced down the side road, hoping to cut you off."

The exit for the highway loomed ahead.

"Well, you caught me," he said. "Now what?"

"I'm coming with you to the cottage," Zoe said. "Alex has briefed Josh and Samantha. They can arrange for me to get back home again."

"Okay." He pulled onto the highway without argument. He didn't know what to say. But he knew he was happy she was there. And that was all that mattered. They drove. Dark summer air rushed through the cracks in the windows. The river ran along the road, as black and smooth as velvet in the night. They turned north and drove through a seemingly endless wall of trees and rocks penning them in on either side.

They drove in silence. Like old friends. Like family. Like "his" and "hers" pillows lying side by side on a headboard. Like a huge dog and a small cat curled up together on the porch in the sunshine. Like how Ivy and Eve would collapse into one chair in a tangle of limbs as if they were one creature with two heads.

At some point, Leo looked down to realize Zoe's hand was tucked safely inside his own. He didn't know whose hand had reached for the other's first, or for how long they'd been holding hands. He squeezed her fingers. She squeezed his back.

A feeling swelled up inside his chest like an ancient beast waking up from a forgotten time, long ago. He felt joy. Joy in the midst of the pain and confusion. For so very long he'd forgotten what it was like to be happy. Now he knew. Sitting here in the darkness, with Zoe holding his hand, was the closest he'd come to perfect happiness in a very long time. If only Ivy and Eve were curled up right now in the back of the truck with them, and the nightmare they were facing as a family was over, his happiness would be complete.

"Thank you for coming with me," he said. "The girls will be so happy to see you. They miss you."

To his surprise her fingers stiffened in his grasp and she pulled away.

"You told me that some people aren't cut out to raise kids." Her voice was quiet in the darkness. "It was pretty clear you meant I was one of them."

"I'm sorry." He tried to grab her hand again, but she'd pulled it back out of his reach. "I was upset because my daughters were in danger."

"The truth is I've always thought you were right," she said. "I wasn't into girlie things like dolls when I was little. Then after the Killian incident, I was in a dark place emotionally and Mom took me for medical tests, and I discovered I'll probably never have kids of my own. Not without a lot of medical procedures, which even then might not work. So I thought, maybe it was because I wasn't a good person for children to be around. I mean, I like combat fighting. I'm a terrible cook. I lost my cool with Killian and fought back, instead of just politely holding my tongue. I told myself I didn't even like children and they didn't like me." She swallowed hard. "Then I met Ivy and Eve."

He cleared his throat. She didn't let him interject.

"Your daughters are amazing," she said. "They're incredible, beautiful and strong. I love them, in this weird, new, fiercely protective way that I never knew was possible to care about another human being. I respect that you want me to stay out of their lives and not complicate what you're all going to be going through. But I promise you, I will do everything in my power to protect them."

He grabbed her hand again. This time she let him hold it.

"Listen to me," he said firmly. "My girls adore you. They think you're amazing. I know I tried to keep you away from them. But that wasn't to protect them. That was to protect me from how I was starting to feel about you."

He took a deep breath and held her hand tighter. Was he really about to admit to Zoe that he was falling in love with her? Was he really about to admit it to himself, here and now, driving through the darkness in the middle of the night while his entire world was collapsing around him?

No, she deserved better than a blurted admission of love that he wasn't able to act on.

"I don't know what to say right now," he said. "I'm just really thankful you're here."

She squeezed him back. "I don't know what to say, either."

He chuckled, a sad, soft sound in the back of his throat. "Then maybe that's how it's going to be."

They kept driving. After a while, Zoe's head fell onto his shoulder and stayed there. Her eyes closed. Her breathing deepened. He bent down and brushed his lips over the top of her head. Eventually, he pulled off the highway and onto the small, private road that would take them to Cedar Lake. The truck slowed. Branches brushed up against the truck, scraping at the paint. Zoe's head bounced lightly against his shoulder as she dozed. Cottage driveways passed his window in the gray of predawn light.

"I don't know what this is between us," Leo whispered in her hair. "Let alone why you landed in my life at the worst possible time. But even though you're asleep and even though this is goodbye, I'm never going to be able to forgive myself if I don't admit, even just to myself, that I never believed it was possible to feel this way about someone until I met you. You're the first. Just you, Zoe. You're my one and only."

The cottage loomed ahead in the darkness. The lake was silent to one side. He cut the engine and slowly ran his hand over Zoe's tousled hair until she roused.

Josh strode down the driveway toward them.

Leo opened the door. "Sorry to wake you."

"Ex-military, light sleeper, comes with the territory," Josh said.

"How are the girls?" Leo asked.

"They're good." Josh yawned. "Stayed up late last night swimming and then a campfire. But they passed out quickly. Samantha's been up ever since Alex called, trying to track down an original source of that letter. But a recent rainstorm is playing havoc on the cell signal and the internet is really slow. Now that you're here, we're thinking of heading across the lake to the Dean family cottage."

"Good idea," Zoe said, hopping out the passenger side. "My parents have a small apartment in the top of their boathouse. After some excitement up here last winter, we set up a really good internet server there, and a small Ash office, so we can stay in better contact."

Leo checked his watch. Sunrise was less than an hour away.

"Sounds good," he said. He wasn't likely to sleep before the girls woke. He wasn't sure he was going to sleep again anytime soon.

Samantha was waiting for them in the doorway of the cottage. He left Zoe to talk to her and Josh, and went upstairs to the second-floor landing. The door to the girls' room was open a crack. He eased it all the way open and stood there in the doorway for a long moment watching his girls sleeping. Eve was curled up on the bed under the skylight, swamped in a mound of blankets so high he could barely see the top of her head. Ivy had kicked her own blankets off and was stretched out on her stomach, in her usual sentry position by her sister's feet, with Fluff the dog stretched out beside her.

Leo sat down in the doorway, leaned back against the frame and watched them sleep. *Ivy, why do you watch guard over your sister while you sleep? What are you afraid of? What can I do to make you ever feel safe again?* His heart ached. The minutes ticked past. He heard Josh and Samantha leave and then the sound of Zoe stretching out on the living room couch. The sun rose slowly, inch by inch, minute by minute, as he kept watch over his children.

After an hour there was a knock on the cottage door. He heard Zoe stir and the babble of voices. But he didn't hear Zoe open the door. The knocking grew louder. He leaped to his feet and started for the stairs. "What's going on? You're going to wake the children."

Zoe stood in the living room, still in her party dress with what he guessed was a pair of Samantha's rolled up yoga pants on underneath. "There's a woman at the door. She says you invited her up but won't produce identification."

"A woman?" He walked past her to the cottage door and looked out. A pair of huge blue eyes stared back. Wisps of blond hair fell around the stranger's face. "Melody?"

Zoe stepped back. "From Marisa's letter?"

"Yes," he said. "We talked on the phone a couple of nights ago about arranging a playdate. I suggested that she and her sons come visit, but Ivy wasn't crazy about the idea."

"Leo?" Worry filled Melody's eyes. "Let me in, please. I saw the letter from Marisa online about the girls. Reporters have been calling me. I want to help."

He glanced past her. A tiny compact car sat in the driveway. There wasn't another person in sight. He eased the door open. "How did you find us?"

"You told me you were heading up to the cottage when we talked on the phone," she said. "The reporter I talked to said this lake was where the cottage was and this was the only place with a light on."

"Which reporter?" Leo asked, even though he knew the answer before she confirmed it. He could only think of one reporter who'd be responding to messages in the middle of the night. "Was it Killian Lynch?"

She nodded. Leo could feel hackles rising on the back of his neck. So Killian had figured out who Zoe was, somehow linked that to the fact her parents had a cottage at Cedar Lake and then told Melody? Who else had he told?

Melody was still smiling at him hopefully.

"I hoped we could sit down like two responsible adults and talk through how best to sort things out for your daughters," she said. She held up a plastic container. "I brought muffins."

"This is very unexpected," he said. Yes, he knew he needed to talk to Melody about the letter. It said Marisa had wanted her to have custody of the girls.

Whether that was true or not, her name was going to be all over the media, too. She was also a casualty in this. It would make all of their lives a lot easier if they could all get on the same page. "I realize it was a long drive and we can talk for a while. But I'm still not ready to tell the girls about the contents of Marisa's letter. I've got someone looking into whether or not it was tampered with or faked. I'd appreciate it if you didn't mention it to the girls, either."

Zoe retreated to the staircase and sat on the steps. He opened the door. Melody walked into the cottage living room and set a plastic container of chocolate chip muffins down on the table. Her blond hair was swept up in a long braid, like Marisa's used to be. Her flowered blouse and skirt could've been picked right out of Marisa's wardrobe.

"Nice to meet you." He shook her hand. It was soft. "This is my friend Zoe."

Melody shook her head and frowned in confusion, as her gaze swept over Zoe's disheveled hair and unusual getup. Zoe stared back at her. For a moment it was like a window had opened in time and Marisa herself was peering through it. It was like Marisa herself was there in the room, meeting Zoe, judging him for falling for her and looking down on him for no longer being the responsible, sensible, cautious man who'd been the father of her daughters.

"What's going on with you?" Melody's voice grew sharp. "Who's she? I thought you agreed you needed a motherly influence in your daughters' lives."

Something in her tone made it crystal clear that Melody had seen herself as applying for the job.

"No!" A sudden cry filled the air—young and desperate. He looked up. Ivy was standing on the landing, still in her pajamas. She pointed at Melody. "Not her! You promised me I didn't have to see her!"

"Ivy!" Leo turned. "That's enough. Melody is just visiting. She wants to help us."

"No." Ivy shook. Fear and fury swept over her tiny frame, laced with a panic that shot him in the heart. Her eyes latched on Melody. "I will never go with you! Stay away from me and Eve!"

Leo felt his own limbs tremble. *Lord, have I been wrong? What have I missed?* Ivy turned and ran for the bedroom, slamming the door so hard it shook. An unfamiliar hand touched his arm and stroked it. He recoiled under the touch.

"She's just a child," Melody said. Her voice was soft and soothing. She reached for his arm again. "She'll get used to it when she realizes it's what's best for her."

What's best for her? The words rang hollow in his mind. Zoe stood and walked up the stairs after Ivy. She knocked on the girls' bedroom door.

Listen to her, Leo.

But she won't talk to me!

Then listen to the words she's not saying.

There was a click. The bedroom door had opened. Eve had let Zoe in.

He wished that he and Melody could just sit down and talk about Marisa, whether there was any truth to the letter and, either way, his need to protect the girls. It would make life so much easier if she agreed not to press for custody. And if his very worst fears came true, he needed Melody to agree to let him have visitation rights. But any hope of that faded the moment he saw fear filling his daughter's eyes.

"Ivy can't be allowed to get away with disrespecting me like that," Melody said. "I won't stand for it. I always told Marisa that one was a little terror who had a serious attitude problem."

"I need you to leave," Leo said. "We can talk again another time, when the girls aren't around. But not like this and not while Ivy's this upset. I need to go talk to my daughter, and you need to go."

It was like a switch had flipped inside Melody's mind. A wall of noise greeted him, much like the constant sound that had hit his ears when he talked to her on the phone the other night. But instead of cheerful, this was angry, indignant, cajoling and threatening all at once. He'd never been a good husband to Marisa, she said, and the girls were better off living with her. But all her words seemed to blend together in an incoherent torrent of sound and fury.

"I'm sorry, you have to go." He held up a hand. "I need to go talk to my daughters. Alone. Feel free to pour yourself a cup of coffee and freshen up if you need to. But when I get back down I expect you to be gone. We can talk on the phone. I will meet with you in mediation. I will follow the law. But my top priority is going to be keeping my girls safe, whether that's convenient or not."

He turned and walked upstairs, leaving her standing there in the living room, her mouth agape. *Lord, why this? Why now? What do I do?* The girls' bedroom door was locked. He knocked on it gently. Eve opened it. She stood there alone in her pajamas, her eyes wide and Fluff clutched tightly in her arms.

"Where are Ivy and Zoe?" he asked.

Eve pointed to the skylight high in the ceiling. A single chair sat beneath it.

"Ivy ran away. She begged me to go with her. But I couldn't reach." Tears filled her eyes. "Zoe went after her."

THIRTEEN

Ivy was crying. Zoe could hear her scared, angry sobs on the far side of the cottage roof. Carefully she crept across the shingles toward the sound, praying as she went. Then she saw her curled into a ball next to the chimney, still in her pajamas with a pair of battered sneakers on her feet.

"Hey, Ivy," she said softly. Gingerly Zoe made her way across the cottage roof toward her. "Okay if I join you?"

Ivy nodded. She sat on the roof beside her and watched as the sun rose slowly through the treetops.

"I was going to run away." Ivy looked up at her with tearstained eyes. "But I can't go without Eve."

"You're a good big sister," Zoe said. "My big brother, Alex, is like that. We always have each other's backs. When my mom died and it was just Dad and me, I was worried that if our lives ever changed it would make things worse. When I met my new mom she turned out to be very different than me, but still really cool. And Alex became my best friend. He told me to come up here with your dad to see you."

"Eve's still little. She doesn't understand a lot of

things so I have to protect her. And adults aren't always good at listening." Ivy looked up at her, her eyes sincere and pleading. "You can't let Melody take Eve away again. You have to protect her!"

Ivy's voice broke. Fresh tears filled her eyes.

"What do you mean, Ivy? Did Melody try to take Eve before?"

"I can't tell you." Her shoulders hunched and she buried her face in her knees. "I'm not supposed to talk about it. Please don't be angry with me."

Suddenly Zoe saw herself, small and tiny, crying in the locker room time and again after Killian had baited and berated her in secret, worried she couldn't tell anyone and that no one would believe her.

"I'm not angry at you," Zoe said. Her arm slid around Ivy's shoulder. She held Ivy close. "I know what it's like to be upset, scared and angry. I know what it's like to think nobody will believe you and not know what to do."

And to do something stupid because she was scared and in over her head.

"Melody moved in next door when I was seven and Eve was three," Ivy said. "She came over a lot and gave us a lot of attention and presents. Especially Eve. She tried to be just like Mommy." She shuddered through her tears. "Sometimes when Mommy wasn't in the room she'd say things. She said Daddy was a bad man and we couldn't trust him, because men like Daddy are bad. She said she loved a man like Daddy once, in the navy, but he hurt her, and she lost her two little twin boys. She said it was all my daddy's fault, so she wanted two little girls like Eve and me to replace them."

"That sounds scary," Zoe said. She held her closer.

"Then one night Mommy went out and left us alone with Melody. We were supposed to go to bed, but Melody told us we were going on a trip far away where Mommy and Daddy would never see us again. I said no. But she picked up Eve and took her to the car." Hysterical tears started pouring down Ivy's cheeks. "She grabbed my hand but I fought her. I tried to stop her from taking Eve, but I wasn't strong enough. She took Eve and left. I hid in the closet and called 9-1-1. Then Mommy came home with the police and Eve came back. Melody said she'd only taken Eve for ice cream and that I'd been rude. Mommy promised me that I'd never have to see Melody again after that. But then Mommy died and I slept in Eve's room so nobody could ever take her again."

"I believe you," Zoe said. She brushed the tears from Ivy's face. "Your daddy will believe you, too. We will do everything we can to protect you and make sure nobody will try to hurt you or Eve again."

Ivy swallowed hard. Then her arms flew around Zoe's neck so suddenly, and hugged her so deeply that for a moment Zoe was almost afraid she was going to tumble down off the roof.

"Zoe's right." A firm, strong voice floated over the roof. She looked up. Leo was sticking his head out the skylight. Zoe's eyes met his over Ivy's head. He mouthed, "Thank you."

Ivy turned toward her dad. "Really?"

"Yes, really!" Protective love for his daughter filled the father's eyes. "I'm sorry I didn't understand before. But I told Melody to leave. And I'm going to do everything I can to protect you now."

He reached up through the skylight, stretching his arms toward Ivy. She crawled across the roof, grabbed his hands and buried her head in her father's arms. He helped Ivy gently through the hole. Zoe heard the sound of Eve diving excitedly into Ivy's arms, and then Leo telling his girls he loved them.

But Zoe stayed on the roof, alone. She stared out at her family's cottage on the other side of the lake and hugged her knees to her chest.

Lord, I never knew it was possible to love anyone the way I love Leo and his daughters. Please protect them. Please give them all the happiness they deserve. Please help me know how to say goodbye to them.

Trees rustled to her right like the wind of an approaching storm. She looked down. A group of men in fatigues were walking through the forest toward the cottage. They were carrying guns.

"Leo, we have a situation."

He looked up as Zoe dropped through the skylight and back into the girls' bedroom. He was crouched on the floor with one arm around each daughter. But in a glance he could tell that they were in trouble. He pulled away from his daughters gently and stood up. Then he leaned close enough to Zoe that she could whisper in his ear.

"We've got hostiles," she whispered. Her hand brushed his arm. "They're in fatigues and carrying weapons. My guess is Eastern European."

Leo's eyes met hers. "How many?"

"At least six. Maybe more."

"Masks?" he asked. She shook her head. So it was a hit squad: brazen, unafraid of being seen and deadly.

The drug smugglers had somehow found him. He'd known this was a risk when he agreed to take on the mission to intercept the smuggling data. But the mission had failed. He'd never retrieved the intel. Yet somehow they must think he had and were now willing to do whatever it took to get it. His eyes rose to the pale light filtering in through the skylight above. He could feel Zoe by his side, and Ivy and Eve by his feet. *Help me, Lord, I need to save them.*

"Can you get to the truck?" he asked.

Zoe shook her head. "No, it's a terrible road, and they have it blocked. No signal on my cell phone, either, but even then it'll take police half an hour to get here. Our only hope is to get to the speedboat and head across the lake to Josh. The girls will be safe there."

The doorknob rattled. Then they heard loud banging against the bedroom door.

"You're running out of time," Melody shouted. "Some bad people are coming, and I can't stop them."

"Call them off, Melody." Leo's voice rose. "We can still end this peacefully. Nobody needs to get hurt."

"I didn't call them!" Her voice rose with a wail of desperation that told him she was telling the truth. "They won't listen to me. I hired The Anemoi to help get me custody of the girls. That's all. But they double-crossed me. They said they found out you're some kind of spy who has information about drug routes, so they sold information about you to organized crime. The Anemoi told me I have until sunrise to leave the cottage with the girls. Then a gang's going to break down the doors, take you and kill anyone who gets in the way."

Who was this woman? Why had she hired The

Anemoi to destroy his family? But his desire for answers collided with the knowledge that the girls were right there, clinging to him, able to hear every word. There were some things he needed to protect them from hearing. A gun blast shook the room as Melody fired into the wall. The girls screamed. He had to get them out of here.

"Take the girls to safety." Leo's eyes locked on Zoe. "You can go through the skylight and run through the woods to the dock. The trees will give you cover. I'll stay here and try to buy you some time. Hopefully they won't notice you're gone until it's too late."

"I can't leave you here," she said.

"Yes, you can," he said. "I won't fit through the skylight and it's the only way to keep the girls safe. Please, Zoe, rescue my girls. I need you to save them."

A second blast sounded. The bullet hit the doorway. Wood splintered around them.

"Girls, go with Zoe." Leo crouched down and pulled both girls close to him. "Go quickly and quietly. Do exactly what she tells you to. I love you, and I'll join you as soon as I can."

He picked both girls up in his arms at once, whispering prayers for their safety. Then he lifted them each in turn through the skylight. They scrambled onto the roof. Their worried faces peered down at him. He turned to Zoe. "Your turn."

"Hang on." Her eyes darted around the room, and then she dove toward the bed, reached underneath and pulled out a small, bundle of fur. She cradled Fluff to her chest. "Okay, now I'm ready."

Gasps of relief echoed down from the girls above. Emotion swelled in his heart. He yanked his sweatshirt off and draped it around her like a sling, tying the puppy against her chest. Then Leo swept Zoe up into his arms. His lips brushed hers, and then he lifted her up above his head. She climbed onto the roof beside his daughters.

A third blast shot through the door, sending wood flying. Melody's aim was getting better. Above him he could hear Zoe and the girls crawling across the roof. He pressed himself against the bedroom wall and waited. Another blast, this one taking out the door handle.

The door swung open. He leaped through the doorway and onto the landing. In one clean, swift motion he knocked the gun from Melody's hands.

"Who are you, really?" He pushed her against the wall. His gaze searched her crazed eyes as he tried to put together the pieces of the terrible story Ivy had told on the roof with everything that The Anemoi had done. "Why did you stalk Marisa and terrorize my girls five years ago? Why did you hire The Anemoi? Why are you trying to steal my daughters?"

"Because you stole my family from me!" Melody spat. "You destroyed my fiancé's life and career! You turned him into a monster and made him do things he wouldn't have done, like taking my boys from me."

The sound of footsteps above had stopped. Then he heard the clatter of them landing on the roof of the shed. Ivy and his daughters had almost made it to the ground.

"You're Tommy Ferrier's fiancée," he said slowly. "He lost his naval career and went to prison after my friend Josh tipped me off to him smuggling drugs on my ship. He went to jail, dealt drugs, hurt you and

made you miscarry your twins. You blamed me for
losing your family, so you went after mine and tried
to steal the girls from Marisa. But Ivy stopped you.
So, you waited, and when you saw me and the girls
all over the media, you convinced The Anemoi to take
them from me."

A crash in the brush outside dragged his gaze to
the picture windows. He saw Ivy, down on the ground
by the tree line. His heart ached to run to her. Then he
saw Zoe grab her hand and pull her to her feet. Eve
leaped on Zoe's back and held on tightly. They ran
into the trees.

"I hired The Anemoi to kidnap them!" Her voice
rose. "But they failed me. All they wanted to do was
scare you, hurt you and try to trick you into letting
me have them."

"They wanted to destroy my life, make me worry
I couldn't protect them and make me doubt they were
even really mine," he said. "Then you were going to
walk in, with a letter from Marisa, and demand custody of them."

It was a cunning plan. But how foolish they'd been
to think anything in the world, even his own failings
and doubt, would ever stop him from fighting for his
girls.

"They let me down!" Her voice rose to an indignant wail.

His head shook in disgust. The fiancée of the same
small-time drug smuggler he'd kicked off his ship
five years ago had hired a ragtag group of thieves to
destroy his family. Instead, they'd sent violent drug
smugglers after him. Ones who he had no doubt would

be all too willing to torture a military officer for intelligence information.

"Just give me the girls and let me leave. Please. I'll take good care of them. I told you, The Anemoi said if I left before sunrise with the girls I'd be okay. But if I tipped you off they'd kill me and the girls."

She looked up at him, pain and rage filling her eyes. But it was how gullible she was that hit him hardest. How had she convinced herself that taking his children would make her whole after the pain of losing hers? Had Tommy's cruel treatment of her damaged something inside her brain or had she been twisted inside from the start?

"I'm going to let you go, and you're going to run." He pulled her to her feet and walked her toward the stairs. "If you stay here, they'll kill you. You need help."

"Not without your girls. If I don't walk out with your daughters those men are going to storm this cottage and kill you."

"I know," he said. He tore two strips of fabric from the bottom of his shirt. Then firmly but not unkindly, he used one to tie Melody's mouth and another her wrists. He did it partly in the hope it would save her life, because it would signal to the criminals outside that she hadn't cooperated with him. But it was also because he needed her to stop fighting him and go. The strips were thin enough that she'd be able to tear them off with some effort, but hopefully not before she'd gotten far away from there. He walked her down the stairs. "Run! Don't stop until you find help. Go! It might be too late for your fiancé. But it's not too late for you."

Gunfire rattled the trees. Melody hesitated, then ran for the door. He ran back up the stairs, his heart wrenching as he saw the scene unfolding through the glass. Ivy was running down the dock toward the boat, now clutching the dog. Zoe was pelting after her, with Eve in her arms. Ivy dove into the boat. Zoe dropped Eve in after her. The girls pressed their bodies against the bottom of the boat. Zoe struggled to untie the rope. Then a tall, blond figure stepped onto the dock. It was Jason. He raised a gun toward Zoe. She dropped the rope and raised her hands. Zoe and the girls were trapped.

The window shattered, destroying his view. Smoke grenades smashed through the cottage. Leo ran for the stairs. The enemy had breached the cottage.

FOURTEEN

Zoe stood on the dock, her hands raised, as she watched Jason walk down the boards toward her. Behind her, she could hear the girls quivering in the bottom of the boat.

"Stop!" Jason aimed a gun between her eyes. "You can't leave yet."

If she leaped into the boat and tried to drive off, he could shoot at the boat and sink it before they were even halfway across the lake. If she dove into the water and tried to make it to the trees, she'd be leaving the girls alone with a criminal. There was no escape. She took a step forward, placing herself between the girls and Jason. This was where she was making her last stand. This was where she was going to fight to protect the two precious girls now hiding behind her even if it cost her her life.

Voices shouted in the woods behind them. Men with weapons were running toward them. Jason's head turned. She rushed him and went for the weapon. She wrestled him for the gun, the weapon mere inches from her face, waiting at any moment to hear the spray of gunfire erupting. But the bullets never came. Her fist caught him in the jaw. The hilt of his gun caught her in the sternum. She grabbed the weapon and yanked it from his grasp. Then she planted her feet and aimed the barrel at his chest.

"I don't want to shoot you," she said. "I honestly don't. So, you're going to back off now and let us leave."

"Wait!" Jason said. His hands rose. But the fingers of his left hand were clenched. "I'm not your enemy. The gun's not even loaded."

"You're a member of The Anemoi. You threatened Leo. You tried to kidnap me."

"Yes, but I told you I didn't want to hurt you and that was the truth. I did my best to stop Prometheus from shooting you and running you over. And I feel really bad for knocking you down the stairs. That was an accident. I'm not really with The Anemoi. I was only using The Anemoi to get information and then get it to Commander Darius." He opened his left hand slowly. He was holding a flash drive. This was Leo's informant? Not one of the delegates or a member of the press core, but a criminal disguised as a waiter. "My name is Seth Miles. I'm a hacker. I have proof that people in naval intelligence have been working with European drug smugglers."

She gasped. His name was infamous. "You were arrested last year for stealing army secrets. You blew a huge military scandal wide open."

She knew Leo's source might have intel similar to the corruption Seth had exposed. She never imagined it could be Seth himself.

"That's me." He nodded. "And I'm afraid I kind of blew my plea deal by digging this information up and then trying to sell it. But I really was trying to do the right thing, the intel really is legit and I needed the money to escape the country. I'm sorry I pushed you down the stairs. I panicked. I had no idea what The Anemoi was really like. I joined them thinking they were people like me, who were trying to right wrongs. Things got way out of hand. I never expected they'd go after anyone's children or try to tear a family apart. I don't hurt people. I don't hurt kids. I just steal secrets from bad people and try to get them in the right hands. I'm trying to do the right thing."

If so, he still had a long way to go. Glass crashed in the distance. The criminals were in the cottage.

"I have no way to pay you or make good on your deal," she said. "You'd be giving it away for nothing."

"Just take it and go," Seth said. He glanced back over his shoulder. "Everything I know about drug smuggling routes, criminals in navy intelligence, The Anemoi and the money Melody Young paid them to gain custody of Ivy and Eve Darius, is on that drive. I promise I never told The Anemoi who you are, your team or the work you do. Get your colleague Samantha Rhodes to look at what's on this drive. She can verify the encryption. Please, Zoe, if I don't run now they'll kill me."

She snatched it from his hand. Seth took off running through the woods. She hacked the rope free, shoved the boat away from the dock and leaped in. Bullets ricocheted in the trees behind her. Men in fatigues were running through the trees toward them. The girls looked up at her from the floor, wide-eyed and silent. She tried the engine. It didn't catch. She tried it again. The engine started. She pulled away from the dock. The small boat shot out over the water. Gunfire erupted over the water toward them. A bullet dinged against the side of the boat. Water rushed in through the hole. Zoe gritted her teeth and pushed the small boat forward.

"I've got it!" Ivy pushed her hand against the hole to block the flow of water rushing into the boat. Tears rushed to Zoe's eyes. Leo's daughters were so precious and brave. The sound of gunfire faded. She stayed low, pressed her hand protectively against the girls' backs and fixed her eyes on the dock ahead. *Please, Lord, may the boat stay afloat long enough for us to get to safety.*

Then she could see Josh and Samantha on the dock waiting for them. The water was already several inches up to the bottom of the boat. She reached her family cottage. Josh pulled them in, helping first the girls and then the dog onto the dock. Samantha dropped to her knees, pulled Ivy and Eve into her arms, and wrapped giant towels around them.

Josh reached for Zoe's hand and pulled her out of the boat.

"The drug smugglers Leo was trying to expose have infiltrated the cottage," she said. "They have Leo penned in. Get the girls to safety and then call the police, the military and every other favor you can call in."

"On it." Josh nodded.

Eve's hand grabbed her hand. "You're going to go back for Daddy, right?"

"You can't let him fight bad guys alone," Ivy said, so seriously something broke inside her. "He needs you."

Both girls' eyes were on her face. She looked at Josh.

"Our highest priority is keeping these girls safe," she said.

"We will." His hand landed firmly on her shoulder. He pressed a small, waterproof walkie-talkie into her hand. "Go help Leo. The girls will be safe with me. I'll get on the phone and call every bit of firepower I can think of to come to your rescue. I'd suggest we switch roles, but Leo is a fellow military man, we're dealing with foreign criminals and I still have military contacts. I know exactly who to call and I know you'll bring him back safely."

"I will." She slid the walkie-talkie into her pocket, pulled out the flash drive and handed it to Samantha. "A hacker named Seth Miles told me to give this to you. He said you'd be able to verify the origin of the contents. He says it contains all the smuggling intel Leo was after."

Samantha took the flash drive and turned it over in her hand. "I'm not quite sure what to make of the fact that an infamous hacker knows my name."

"I think he knows all our names," Zoe said. "I almost got the impression that he admires what you do, especially since it looks like he was the person you've been matching wits with online."

She wondered if he was serious about trying to be one of the good guys, and what the rest of the team would think if a former criminal ever approached them about joining the team.

"Hang on." Samantha disappeared into the boathouse and returned seconds later with a sealed, waterproof pouch. "Give Leo this. It's the original version of the letter Marisa wrote him. She'd backed it up to an online server. If anything happens, make sure he has it."

Zoe slipped it inside her pocket. "I will."

She crouched down and hugged both girls closely, words failing her lips even before she could speak them. Then she turned, dove cleanly into the water and started swimming.

Leo's energy was flagging. When the smoke bombs had first exploded through the windows, filling the cottage with smoke, he'd focused on staying hidden and finding an exit, while he prayed Zoe and his daughters had made it to safety. He'd retreated to the master bedroom and pressed himself against the wall, listening, praying, waiting as he'd heard the shouts of men swarming the cottage below him and the rhythmic crash of door after door being burst open, and room after room being tossed as the criminals came looking for him.

When they'd reached him, he was ready. He leaped, knocking the criminal off his feet and to the ground, followed by a quick punch to the jaw to make sure he stayed there. But now his cover was blown, the enemy was upon him and there was nothing left to do but fight.

He chose the living room for his final stand, staying low and quick even as the smoke seared his lungs and gunfire erupted around him. He caught a second man in the chest with a flying kick that knocked him to the ground. Then Leo rolled under the cloud of rising smoke as it surged above him. He came up beside another operative, caught him by the shoulder and tossed him into the couch. But as Leo swung back, he was kicked hard from behind. He sprawled to his hands and knees, gritted his teeth and climbed back to his feet.

Leo fought for his life, blow after blow, six on one, as the men around him pummeled him down in an attempt to take him alive. He had no idea where they were planning on taking him for questioning or what they were going to do with him when they got there, but didn't much want to find out.

How many criminals had he taken down, disarming them of their weapons and tearing the guns from their grasp, only to be leaped on by another? He was being overtaken by a swarm.

He rolled onto his knees. Panting. Praying. He would fight until his final breath. He could continue to take down man after man, criminal after criminal until he could take no more. But he couldn't fight forever.

Then he heard the screech of a truck—his truck— and the crash of glass and wood. Sunlight poured through the hole in the wall. He looked up. Someone had driven his truck straight through the window and into the cottage.

"Leo!" A strong and beautiful voice cut through the chaos. "This way!"

It was Zoe. She'd crashed his truck right into the middle of the living room, offering him a means of escape. All he had to do was reach the vehicle, get inside and they could drive out of the fight to safety.

He ran toward her, feeling fresh energy fill his lungs. Men lunged at him on either side. He fought them back. He had to reach her.

Zoe screamed as a large brute of a man grasped her around the neck and yanked her from the truck. Her feet kicked in the air. Her hands clutched her attacker's hands. With a decisive throw, Leo tore Zoe's attacker off her and tossed him to the ground. Zoe fell to her knees. He grabbed her hand and helped her up.

"Where are my girls?"

"Safe." Her hands rose in front of her. "With Josh and Samantha. He's calling for backup."

"Thank You, God!" he prayed.

"Amen."

Leo and Zoe stood back-to-back, protecting each other as criminals rained blows down on them. They reached the truck. Leo grabbed Zoe around the waist and hoisted her into the vehicle.

"You're driving," he shouted. He leaped in the passenger side. "You know Cedar Lake. I don't."

She threw the truck in Reverse. The truck shot backward out the hole in the wall. "I thought you didn't like me driving your truck."

"You already smashed my truck into a cottage," he said. "I don't figure you can do much worse."

"I told you, I only crash when people are shooting at me!"

The truck shot backward up the narrow and curving cottage road. Above, he could hear the whir of helicopters. Sirens echoed in the distance. Zoe spun the truck until they were going forward again and gunned it down a tiny dirt track.

"Josh called everyone," she said. "Fire, ambulance, police, military, every favor he could pull in. Jason of The Anemoi was your informant. He's really Seth Miles. I retrieved the intel and then some. Samantha is processing it now."

She drove a few minutes down a narrow track, then stopped at a cottage. He looked behind him. No one was following them. Emergency services were arriving. They were safe.

He reached for Zoe's hand and squeezed it. She squeezed it back.

"You came back for me," he said.

"Of course I did." She looked down at their hands. "That's what partners do. But to be fair, you took on about a dozen international criminals in hand-to-hand combat. I mostly just provided the getaway vehicle."

"You got my daughters to safety," he said. "And that gave me the strength and power to take on an army of foes. I couldn't have done this without you."

He pulled her toward him. But instead she pushed him back.

"Wait," Zoe said. "I care about you and about your girls, more than I knew it was possible to care about anyone. But we still have real life to worry about and I have something you need to open."

She pressed something against his chest. He looked down. It was a waterproof pouch.

"It's the letter from Marisa," she said. "The original one. Samantha was able to download it from an online server."

He took it from her. She slipped from his arms, opened the front door of the truck and jumped out.

"Read it," she said, "and then tell me what our next move is. Because whatever we think and whatever we feel can't get in the way of protecting the girls."

FIFTEEN

Zoe slipped out of the truck, leaving Leo alone. To her right, she could see the flashing lights. She reached for the walkie-talkie in her pocket.

"Zoe!" Samantha's voice crackled in her ear.

"It's me. We're safe and fine at the Mullocks' cottage."

"Is that Zoe?" Eve's voice practically yipped. "Can I talk to her?"

Zoe smiled. "Hi, Eve, yes it's me. Is Ivy there with you, too?"

"Yeah," Ivy said. "Are you with Daddy? Did you get away?"

"Yes, I'm safe with your daddy," she said. Zoe sat down on the edge of the dock, closed her eyes and let the girls' voices fill her heart. "In fact, I'm calling to see if you guys can come pick us up."

Due to the way Cedar Lake curved, the cottage was thirty minutes away by truck. But by boat, Josh could be there in eight.

Samantha said, "Joshua says we're on our way."

"Fluff is asleep in your dog's bed," Ivy said, her voice ever serious. "I hope that's okay."

"I'm sure Oz won't mind at all." Zoe smiled.

"The boathouse has bunk beds!" Eve's voice filled the airwaves. "Can we stay here tonight?"

"It's up to your daddy."

"Will you stay here, too, at the lake with us?" Eve asked. "Josh and Samantha can stay, too. And Alex and Theresa. There are lots of rooms. You could go get your dog to keep Fluff company."

Tears of sadness and joy mingled together suddenly in Zoe's eyes. "I don't know, honey. But I'm sure your daddy would be happy to have some time at the cottage with you."

Footsteps on the dock behind her made her pause. She turned and looked up. Leo was walking slowly down the dock toward her. She held the walkie-talkie out toward him. But instead he shook his head and held up a finger to his lips.

"Okay, I've got to go," she said to the girls. "I'll see you when you get here. Over and out."

She switched the walkie-talkie off. Leo reached down a hand, grabbed her and pulled her to her feet.

"I was just talking to Eve and Ivy," she said. "They're excited to see you."

"I can't wait to see them. But first, I need to read you something." Leo brushed a finger gently over her lips. "I need you to be quiet and not interrupt or talk until I'm done. Okay?"

She nodded. He pulled his finger away from her lips, took her hand and led her over to a bench by the water. They sat.

"As you know, Samantha found Marisa's original letter," he said. "In some ways, it's harder to read than the fake one Melody had The Anemoi create to help her steal custody of my girls. She forgives me for the problems in our marriage and asks for my forgiveness, too. We both made a lot of mistakes and there's a lot here I wish we could've said to each other when she was alive. Maybe if I hadn't been overseas things might have been different, I don't know." He took a deep breath in, and let it out again. "She does mention Melody, but only as someone who'd scared Ivy once by leaving her home alone when she was supposed to be watching the girls. She looked into getting a restraining order against her, but Melody disappeared so she never pressed it. I don't think she ever had any idea how dangerous she really was—"

"And the girls?" Zoe asked.

"They're mine," Leo said. He laughed. "She doesn't say anything at all about them not being mine and in fact mentions several times how grateful she is that I'm the man who fathered her children. She thinks we made beautiful children."

Zoe smiled. "You did."

Leo reached around her waist and pulled her up onto his lap. "Since you seem incapable of not interrupting, how about you read this final part?"

She nestled into the strength of his arm and looked down at where he was pointing.

"Finally," she read aloud.

"Leo, I want you to be happy. I want you to forgive yourself and forgive me for the mistakes of our past. I want you to let go of guilt. I know I once made you promise that if anything ever happened to me, you wouldn't consider any other relationships until the girls were grown. That was my fear and pain talking.

"But now that I'm gone, I want you to go find love. Find a woman who loves you, who makes you happy, who fills your heart with joy and makes you the man God wants you to be. Find a woman who will love our girls and be a second mother to them. That is my final prayer for you, dear Leo. Find happiness. Find joy. Find love. Be happy.
Thank you for everything,
Marisa"

Her words faded. He pulled the letter from her hands.

"I'm ready to be happy, Zoe," he said. "What makes me happy is you. I don't know why I needed Marisa to point it out to me, but she's right. I'm ready to start again. You fill my heart with joy. I had no idea love could feel like this." He slid his hands along her back. His fingers tangled in her hair. "I'm in love with you, Zoe. I don't know what happens next or how long it will take to put this whole nightmare behind us. But I know I want you to be a part of my life and part of the girls' lives. I know that I now have hope for the future again, because of you."

She looked up at him. "I love you, too."

His lips found hers. He kissed her deeply and firmly. Then he let her go and, holding tightly to her hand, they ran down the dock together to greet the girls.

EPILOGUE

"Look at me, Zoe! Watch me!" Eve called. "I'm making it rain two colors of flowers at once!"

Zoe looked up at the tree above her head, as both pink and white flower petals showered down around her. Eve hung upside down from the tree above her in the sparkling dress she'd worn to Alex and Theresa's wedding. "Did you ever see one tree that could grow two flowers?"

"I think it's two types of trees that grew together," Zoe said. "Is this what you needed me to see?"

"Wait," Eve called. "I need to climb even higher for it to really work!"

Zoe laughed and looked out over Cedar Lake. Alex and Theresa's wedding had been beautiful and elegant, held on the site of the new cottage that the happy couple were in the process of building. It had been a small event, with only a few friends, family members and neighbors from the lake, coming together for a simple potluck. Now the event was done. Most people had gone home. But before Zoe could help with cleaning up, Eve had grabbed her by the hand and dragged her away to show her this special tree.

Late May sunshine glinted on the lake. Another spring had ended and another summer was about to begin. It had been almost a year since The Anemoi had threatened Leo and the girls. Seth was in the wind again, but his intel had proved true and thanks in no small part to Leo's work, the drug network was being dismantled. Admiral Jacobs had been very pleased with the additional data that naval intelligence had gleaned by interrogating the foreign criminals that had been captured following the attack on the cottage. Melody had been arrested, too, and was getting the help she needed.

Leo had decided to resign from the military to work with Ash Private Security. Zoe had continued to spend time with Leo and his girls, slowly and gently growing into each other's lives, entangled together, like the branches of the half cherry and half crab apple tree, raining down flowers above her head

"Now watch," Eve commanded. "You are watching, right?"

Zoe laughed again. "I'm watching."

"Catch me, I'm a flower!" Eve dropped from the tree and into Zoe's arms, a giggling mess of happiness, flower petals and sunshine. Zoe kissed her head and set her on the ground.

"You've got something in your hair." A deep voice made her look up. Leo was coming through the trees toward her. Ivy was by his side, with Oz held firmly under one arm and Fluff under the other. Both dogs were in large sparkling bows.

"I'm sure I have a lot of things in my hair," Zoe said, as Leo reached down and plucked out petals. "Eve made the tree rain."

Eve giggled and scampered back up the path toward the cottage with Ivy. The girls and dogs disappeared into the trees.

"Come on," Leo said. "Alex and Theresa want to say goodbye to you before they leave for their honeymoon." He slipped his hand into Zoe's. They walked up the path. "Ivy and Eve love you so much."

"I love them, too," Zoe said. "Getting to know you all is the best thing that's ever happened to me."

Leo pulled her tighter to his side. "You're the best thing that could've possibly happened to us."

A giggling cry cut through the trees.

"Zoe!" Eve called. "Help!"

Zoe gripped Leo's hand. They ran, pushing through the branches. The trees parted and they saw Eve and Ivy standing on the top balcony of the cottage shouting Zoe's name. Alex, Theresa, Samantha and Josh ran out onto the balcony toward them, their arms filled with wedding gifts. Zoe's mind whirled. Why were the girls shouting? What was going on? Theresa was carrying a large, colorfully decorated cardboard box. Before Zoe even had time to think, it slipped and fell from the new bride's hands. The box tumbled over the edge of the balcony and down toward the ground below.

"Zoe! Catch it!" Ivy yelled.

Zoe dropped Leo's hand and dove for it, her fingertips clasping over it inches before it hit the ground. She rolled back to her feet and held it up. It was remarkably light.

"Got it!" Zoe called. She looked up. Why were the girls giggling? The box fell open. It was Theresa's wedding bouquet.

Zoe looked up. Theresa was smiling apologetically.

Alex was laughing into his hand. Josh was grinning. Samantha was smiling behind the lens of a camera. Ivy and Eve were practically leaping up and down with joy.

"She caught the wedding bouquet, Daddy!" Eve shouted. "She caught the wedding bouquet! Now you have to get married."

Leo chuckled. He reached for her hand. "Well, if we have to, I guess we have to."

"You set this up." Zoe looked at him in surprise, then up to her loved ones, clustered on the balcony. "You all set me up!"

"Don't hold it against them," Leo said softly. "Think of it as mobilizing the entire team to achieve a singular objective."

She shook her head. "You're terrible."

"I love you." Leo dropped to his knees at her feet. "I started falling in love with you that first moment we met. I've been falling deeper and deeper in love with you every moment since then. Please marry me."

Above her, Zoe could hear the excited shrieks and giggles of the girls she'd grown to love. But her eyes locked on Leo.

"This is the part where you say yes," he whispered. His eyebrows rose. "My girls and I won't feel complete without you."

"Yes, of course I'll marry you!" She laughed and he pulled a small ring box from his pocket, opened it and revealed a ring with three stones. The diamond in the center was ringed by an emerald on one side and a sapphire on the other, for the small family of three that had stolen her heart and invited her to join them.

"You didn't have to go to all this trouble," she whispered as he slid it onto her finger. "I would've agreed to marry you over a slice of pizza while sitting on the couch."

"I know," he said. "But where would the fun have been in that?"

Then he swept her up into his arms and spun her around.

"She said yes!" he shouted.

"Of course I did!" Zoe shouted.

Then they kissed as cheering erupted above them and fresh flower petals rained down around them.

* * * * *

If you enjoyed Protective Measures, *look for the other books in the* TRUE NORTH BODYGUARDS *series:*

KIDNAPPED AT CHRISTMAS
RESCUE AT CEDAR LAKE

Dear Reader,

When was the last time you did something that scared you? I've never written a book about children before this one. Honestly, I've always been intimidated by the thought of creating small fictional children and letting them run loose on the page. But I wrote this over the summer, when my own girls were home from school, and they encouraged me to bring Ivy and Eve to life.

Like Zoe, I was once told I'd never have children, and while that turned out not to be the case, that moment is still sharp in my memory. Like both Leo and Zoe, I've had plenty of days worrying that I wasn't as good a parent as I wanted to be. I'm so thankful to my girls for helping me find strength and courage I never knew I had.

Thank you again to all the amazing readers who've gotten in touch with their thoughts, questions and suggestions about the characters and their stories. The best place to reach me is on Twitter at @MaggieKBlack or through my website, www.maggiekblack.com. I really do love hearing what you think. Several of you wrote to ask me what Seth from *Tactical Rescue* was up to now, and I was glad when Leo and Zoe's brush with espionage gave a little bit of a hint into that.

Also, Arwen wrote to ask what had happened to the cat in *Kidnapped at Christmas*. The cat is doing great. Samantha found it when she was moving out of her apartment. It's now very happy living with her and Josh, and often curls up on the chair beside her when she's reading.

Thank you all for sharing this journey with me,
Maggie

Get 2 Free Books,
Plus 2 Free Gifts—
just for trying the *Reader Service!*

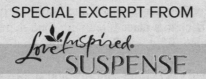
If the Everglades didn't kill her, her uncle would.

Either way, Esme Dupree was going to die.

The thought of that—of all the things she'd leave behind, all the dreams she'd never see come true—had kept her moving through the Florida wetlands for three days, but she was tiring. Even the most determined person in the world couldn't keep running forever. And she'd been running for what seemed nearly that long. First, she'd fled witness protection, crisscrossing states to try to stay a step ahead of her uncle's henchman. She'd finally found her way to Florida, to the thick vegetation and quiet waterways that her parents had loved.

Esme wasn't as keen. Her family had spent every summer of her childhood in Florida exploring the wetlands. She preferred open fields and prairie grass, but her parents had loved the shallow green water of the Everglades. She'd never had the heart to tell them that she didn't.

Funny that she'd come back here when her life was falling apart. When everything she'd worked for had been

shot to pieces by her brother's and uncle's crimes, Esme
had come back to a place filled with fond memories.

It was also filled with lots of things that could kill a
person.

She wiped sweat from her brow and sipped water from
her canteen. Things hadn't been so bad when she'd been
renting a little trailer at the edge of the national park. She'd
had shelter from the bugs and the critters. But Uncle Angus
had tracked her down and nearly killed her. He would have
killed her if she hadn't smashed his head with a snow globe
and called the police. They'd come quickly.

Of course they had.

They were as eager to get their hands on her as Uncle
Angus had been.

"You should have stayed with the police," she muttered.
Maybe she would have if Angus's hired guns hadn't
firebombed the place. She'd run again because she thought
she'd be safer on her own.

Now she wasn't so sure.

Don't miss
BODYGUARD by Shirlee McCoy,
available wherever
Love Inspired® Suspense books and ebooks are sold.

www.LoveInspired.com

LISEXP0717

Love Inspired®

Inspirational Romance to Warm Your Heart and Soul

Join our social communities to connect with other readers who share your love!

Sign up for the Love Inspired newsletter at **www.LoveInspired.com** to be the first to find out about upcoming titles, special promotions and exclusive content.

CONNECT WITH US AT:

Harlequin.com/Community

 Facebook.com/LoveInspiredBooks

Twitter.com/LoveInspiredBks